G. B. Szymanski is a 1968 graduate of The Citadel, The Military College of South Carolina, a former U.S. Air Force captain, a Vietnam veteran, and a retired Federal Aviation Administration air traffic control supervisor. This work of fiction is based on his own personal experience, as well as on the experiences of those with whom he proudly served.

Dedicated to my grandchildren and to my alma mater,
The Citadel, Class of 1968.

G. B. Szymanski

FOLLOW WITHOUT FEAR

AUSTIN MACAULEY PUBLISHERS™

LONDON • CAMBRIDGE • NEW YORK • SHARJAH

Ordering Information:
Quantity sales: special discounts are available on quantity purchases by corporations, associations, and others. For details, contact the publisher at the address below.

Publisher's Cataloging-in-Publication data
Szymanski, G. B.
Follow Without Fear

ISBN 9781643786780 (Paperback)
ISBN 9781643786797 (Hardback)
ISBN 9781645364849 (ePub e-book)

The main category of the book — FICTION / Romance / Historical / 20th Century

Library of Congress Control Number: 2019910941

www.austinmacauley.com/us

First Published (2019)
Austin Macauley Publishers LLC
40 Wall Street, 28th Floor
New York, NY 10005
USA

mail-usa@austinmacauley.com
+1 (646) 5125767

A special thanks to my lovely wife, Joanne, and lovely daughter, Erica, for their encouragement and support during the creation of this work.

Time! What an empty vapor 'tis!
And days, how swift they are!
Swift as an Indian arrow flies,
Or like a shooting star.

The present moments just appear,
Then slide away in haste;
That we can never say, "They're here,"
But only say, "They're past."

— Isaac Watts

Foreword

Stan was now in his seventies. He was relaxing on the front porch of his Texas home with his lovely wife of almost fifty years and their dog, Charlie. The air was turning crisp as autumn made its entrance, and the leaves on the cedar elm trees flanking either side of the house were turning from green to shades of orange and yellow. Their young grandson was playing with a ball on the lawn in front of them when a low-flying plane appeared overhead. The sound of the plane interrupted their solitude and brought back memories of youth and hope, and a loss too painful to bear. His wife shivered, and he did not have to look at her to see there were tears in her eyes.

The road they had taken was similar to that traveled by so many young people of their generation. They were called upon by their leaders and heroes to perform in accordance with expectations. Many did not heed that call, but many others did. The country was divided and its youth paid the price.

One

Ready

1

The year was 1964. He was stunned. The rifle suddenly flew from his grip as he stood with his squad at a parade rest position. Thunderous, mind numbing sounds with unfamiliar southern drawls then assaulted his ears as cadet corporals administering punishment placed their lips so close to his ears that an increase in temperature and moisture became apparent even though he was being drilled and grilled, along with others, in hot, humid, August, South Carolina sunshine. Stan knew that he should not move and not say a word. His research prior to entering the plebe system at the military college taught him that his only permissible responses were "yes sir," "no, sir," and "no excuse, sir." And those responses were only permitted when he was asked a question by a higher-ranking cadet. So far, he was only being admonished and he was not permitted to speak. The infraction, just one of many to come, was not gripping his weapon tight enough to remain in his grasp and withstand the swift kick it suffered from a cadet corporal. To reinforce his message, the corporal instructed the plebe to sleep with his rifle tucked in his bunk that night, and the corporal checked on the cadet plebe that evening to ensure his instructions had been followed.

During the little free time he had throughout this initial military training, Stan frequently questioned his reasons for having chosen to attend such a demanding college. He was, after all, a Yankee from northern New Jersey with an accent revealing his roots. It took some time and effort before he could really understand what occasionally sounded like a foreign language. Having graduated in the top ten percent of his high school class, with acceptance letters from three other colleges offering similar courses of study and ROTC programs, why on earth did he choose this school?

The ravings and rantings of Senator Joe McCarthy during the 1950s were still very much part of American culture. Stan's dad, teachers, friends, and coaches saw communists behind all vegetation large enough to conceal such clandestine individuals. He had been taught how Russian government officials spied on their citizens, arrested, imprisoned, and sometimes tortured anyone daring to speak out against their social order. His dad was very much a part of the anti-communist John Birch following and he admired everything about his father.

As was the case for most working class families, college expenses for the children meant sacrifice for the entire family. His father's goal was to ensure that every one of them received the best education he could possibly provide. And his sons all worked part-time jobs during their high school years while presenting him with their pay to help defray future college expenses.

Many of his closest friends enlisted in branches of the military following high school graduation rather than enter the ranks of factory workers, truck drivers, store clerks and other types of labor performed by their parents. Unlike his friends, he attempted to escape such an existence by gaining entry into one of the federal military academies. After applying and taking examinations, he had been placed on a list as a secondary appointee to the Merchant Marine Academy at Kings Point, New York. This meant that, in the event the primary appointee was unable to attend, Stan would be his replacement. However, that did not happen. He also applied and was accepted to The Citadel, The Military College of South Carolina. The young man decided to attend; however, his parents would have to pay tuition. That school was known for its extremely difficult training environment. There were those at home who said he would never make it through such an ordeal, and he felt added pressure to succeed as a result.

Stanley Marks would turn eighteen in three weeks. He was now at the college he had chosen to attend, and vowed that he would never leave without a degree and a commission as a second lieutenant in the United States Air Force. He worked hard and endured every hardship thrown his way for four, long, grueling years. Later in life, after much reflection, he would thank his parents for their strict upbringing. They, along with teachers, relatives, coaches, and clergy gave him the foundation necessary to accomplish that goal. His military school training prepared him well for what was to follow and it was now time to seek out additional challenges.

Following graduation, the newly commissioned Air Force officer was assigned to Keesler Air Force Base in Biloxi, Mississippi for air traffic control training. During a six-week hiatus between commencement and his first assignment, he worked for a state-sponsored summer school program designed for disadvantaged youth. Earnings from that job allowed him to make a down payment on a used sports car, which would take him from New Jersey to Mississippi.

Fortunately, he had, by this time, developed an excellent ear for southern accents and had pretty well lost his distinctive New Jersey twang. That would prove to serve him well for a long time to come. He loved his 1967, Pontiac Firebird. That was the first year Pontiac produced this model and it was his freedom machine. The Firebird was candy apple red with a black vinyl roof, a black interior, black air intake scoops on the hood, and black racing stripes along its sides. It had a 325 horsepower V-8 engine and more chrome under the hood than on the exterior of the vehicle. The car was not air-conditioned, but few were in those days. This young man had never lived in air-conditioned comfort and rolling down the window for fresh air was all he needed and all he wanted. The feel of wind blowing through his well-cropped military-style hair put a smile on his face and a glow in his heart. He was finally beginning to live his dream.

He was free from his humdrum, blue-collar New Jersey existence and free from the rigors of military school; he was on his way at last. Now a second lieutenant in the United States Air Force, he already considered himself a successful man. He had made it and was looked up to by his friends, family, and relatives. Before leaving home for Mississippi, the young officer had opportunity to smile at those who said he would never survive the demands of a military college; several shook his hand and wished him well. A good lesson was learned. People tend to admire and respect those who overcome adversity and to shun those who admit failure and quit. Stan was now a certified survivor and a determined young man. During his cadet career, he watched many fall by the wayside and never complete the program. All of his relatives who served in the military during the world war did so as enlisted personnel and they were proud of the officer in the family. He was determined to see that continue.

2

As Stan travelled around Washington D.C. to the countryside of Virginia, he marveled at the majesty and the beauty of the wonderful country he had now committed himself to defend at all costs. He took pride in what he had done and in what he intended to do. The newly minted Air Force officer was offended by the many young people of his generation who did not appear to respect the country's military and its mission in Southeast Asia. Before leaving on this trip, he stopped at a diner with his younger brother, Pat, for a cup of coffee and a brotherly chat. New Jersey was known for its many diners and they were popular places for casual social encounters. Pat was now a cadet at Stan's old military school and intended to make the Marine Corps his career. As they joked about life at The Citadel and enjoyed a few good laughs over common experiences, they were overheard by some of the other people seated close by.

The two young men looked around the diner and suddenly felt uncomfortable. They seemed out of place in their local surroundings even though they had lived there all of their lives. The nineteen and twenty-one year old brothers looked very much like soldiers out of uniform and on leave. Their hair was short and their dress was neat and clean.

Pro and con signals regarding the Southeast Asia War seemed to be everywhere. Other young diners seated nearby were obviously anti-establishment types, with long hair and unconventional attire. The air was thick with bewildering hostility and subliminal messages seemed to be uttering phrases such as 'Support the troops' or 'Hell no, I won't go.' The two brothers realized that they appeared to be in the minority. They were apparently the center of attention, and the group seated nearby seemed strangely interested in their presence and in their conversation.

With ill-concealed disdain, Stan abruptly remarked, "Hey Pat, let's get out of here."

As they paid their bill before leaving the diner, cold stares from some of their contemporaries were obvious, disturbing, and a bit painful. A particularly obnoxious individual made remarks, including phrases such as "baby killers" and "murderers." Pat stopped in his tracks and seemed eager to engage in confrontation. But before he could turn around, Stan grabbed his arm and led him to the door.

Once outside, the older brother said, "Forget it, Pat, it's just not worth it."

These young men had become more than just brothers; they were now best friends and looked up to each other. Pat aspired to be an aviator as well, but he had his eyes set on the Marine Corps for his training. Seems as though the yearning for aviation had been passed on from father to sons, or perhaps it was a goal of his sons to complete the father's unfulfilled dreams.

Stan was the first of his family to ever attend a college. At home were two younger brothers and a sister. They were raised by a severely strict father who did not hesitate to discipline his sons when he believed it was the right thing to do. Respect was demanded and hard work was expected. This occurred during the late 1950s and early 1960s. Their dad had been a child during the Great Depression and was the son of Polish immigrants who Americanized their original surname from Marek to Marks after arrival in the United States.

As a young man during World War II, his father was raised in a northern New Jersey township, where he would walk to the nearby municipal airport to watch airplanes take off and land. His heroes were Charles Lindbergh and Amelia Earhart. As the story was told, he wanted to become a pilot during the war and, at the age of 26, was disappointed to learn he was too old for flight school. At the time, he was employed as a shipfitter at the Brooklyn Navy Yard and his work was needed by the defense department for repairs to the navy's ships. There, he met Stan's mother, a blonde beauty also from northern New Jersey who worked in the supply area. The courtship that began in that shipyard developed into a lasting bond, which produced four towheaded children.

Stan's father was determined to make his three sons tough enough to face the inevitable difficulties he believed they would encounter in life. The daughter was the youngest, the princess to be protected by the rest of the family. As was common at that time, Mrs. Marks became a homemaker after the birth of her first child. She was a strong woman who stood by every member of the family, especially her husband, the hardworking martinet.

Driving through Virginia, Stan thought about the differences in the reactions he had experienced at home since graduation. The disparity was overwhelming and confusing. He was admired and respected on the one hand, yet utterly and completely disdained on the other. What was happening to his country? He took refuge in the fact that his closest friends were of his mind and that those he only considered acquaintances were not. But were we not all Americans? He loved and respected those who had served and fought in America's previous conflicts. What had changed and why?

By the time of his college graduation and military commissioning in 1968, the Vietnam War had become a giant thorn in the nation's side and his beloved country was being torn apart by those for and against the conflict. The United States was also suffering from severe racial tension, and he witnessed the entrance of the first black cadet at his military college, which had previously been an all-white male institution. His boyhood hero, John F. Kennedy, had been killed during his high school years and he was determined to live by JFK's directive to ask not what his country could do for him, but to ask what he could do for his country.

Although Stan occasionally experienced misgivings about his country's policies, he would never voice them. Those feelings generated enormous guilt and he asked himself how he could possibly question leaders of the greatest country on Earth. Those leaders were, only and always, interested in the well-being of all American citizens. He had been taught by the greatest generation of Americans every step of the way during his young life and to question such authority, in effect, questioned everything he had been taught to stand for. If they demanded that we sacrifice for our country, then sacrifice we must.

As the young military officer continued his journey to Mississippi, he intended to stop overnight in North Carolina. His former cadet company commander during his first year at the military college was now an Army infantry captain and a company commander at Fort Bragg. He had not seen Bart Small since Bart's graduation three years earlier and he was looking forward to this reunion. After writing a letter to Captain Small, whom he had located through the alumni association, he was happily surprised to receive a reply asking him to visit on his way to his first Air Force assignment.

The initial portion of his journey to Mississippi terminated upon arrival at a front gate for Fort Bragg. It was about 1730 hours (5:30 p.m.) and still daylight at that time of the year. He checked in with the guard on duty and was directed to a BOQ (Bachelor Officers' Quarters).

When he entered the building, he could hear cheerful bantering and the clinking of billiard balls some distance down a hall. Heading in that direction, a voice became clearly recognizable. It was a voice that had barked commands at his cadet unit for an entire academic year.

That voice put a smile on his face. Upon turning a corner, he observed several young men shooting pool and shooting the breeze between bouts of raucous laughter. His first observation of Bart after three years was his backside as Bart was bent over a pool table about to take a shot. There was no mistaking that it was Bart. He was accustomed to observing his old leader from the rear after a full year of following him in formation as they marched, drilled, jogged, ran through obstacle courses, and sweated through numerous other activities indigenous to military life. He smiled to himself at this observation of his old cadet commander and thought, *We sweat so much as cadets back then. Now that we are officers, I guess we'll just have to learn to perspire.* Bart still had the same severely shaved military head and was in the same excellent physical condition.

Stan stood there a moment and waited for Bart to complete his shot, then barked, "Captain Small, sir, Lieutenant Marks is reporting as ordered, sir." Bart straightened up and very slowly turned around. When he faced Stan squarely, he wore a serious expression and yelled, "God damn it, boy, they'll let anyone become an Air Force officer these days. Are you kidding me? Did you actually graduate? I had my doubts about you, boy."

Bart then smiled broadly and so did Stan, who replied, "You and I both had doubts, sir. But yes, I did graduate and I am an Air Force officer."

They both laughed heartily and opened their arms as they approached each other.

Bart slapped Stan on the back and congratulated him for successfully navigating the many pitfalls encountered during four years at a military college. He seemed pleased to introduce the newly commissioned Air Force officer to his friends, who kidded him playfully. They welcomed Bart's old pal to what was referred to as a real military facility as compared to an Air Force base.

The two young reunited military officers then had dinner and drinks at the base officers' club. It was Stan's first trip to any officers' club and he let Bart know that on their short walk there. The club was a special experience for him. He was impressed. His family did not eat in restaurants and they did not belong to any clubs.

Wow! Do I really belong here? he thought.

They sat at a table and a young waitress approached to take their order. Bart ordered a scotch and water and Stan hesitated. His family did not drink. That was another sacrifice made to help afford college educations for the kids. He did have an occasional beer when on leave with other cadets at military school, but that was the extent of his drinking experience. Then he recalled some other guys drinking something at a football game when he was in high school and he said, "I'll have a rum and coke."

Bart started laughing and Stan, who felt his face turning red, asked, "Why is that funny, sir?"

"Because that's a kid's drink, Lieutenant," answered Bart.

He then turned to the waitress and said, "Bring us two scotch and waters."

"Stan, when you get to that Air Force base of yours, do not order any kid drinks. You are now a man and you'll drink like one," said Bart.

Bart made his point alright and Stan replied, "Yes sir, I'll remember that."

Captain Small also hailed from a New Jersey township and they reminisced about their youthful trips to the Jersey shore. He smiled as Bart recalled week-long family vacations in rented homes at various shore towns and of the great food, games, and rides along the boardwalks.

He listened more than he talked and Bart seemed to enjoy his attentive audience. The captain's stories were a marked contrast to the new lieutenant's family day trips at the beach. He did enjoy romping in the ocean with his younger brothers, but always wondered about the boardwalk amusements. His family packed lunches and entertained themselves playing ball on the beach. Stan promised himself that he would someday stay at a nice hotel or rent a summer home to show his future family a good time. And yes, he would take them on the boardwalk.

Their drinks arrived and Bart ordered them both steak dinners. The Air Force lieutenant gave his dinner companion a surprised look as the waitress moved from the table and the captain announced that the meal and drinks were on him.

"That sure is nice of you, sir," remarked Stan.

"My pleasure, Lieutenant. By the way, there's a room available for you at the BOQ tonight. With all of these overseas deployments lately, our stateside bases are short-staffed as you will soon find out when you get settled in at your first assignment after your initial training."

Stan was incredibly grateful, as it had been a very long day. "You're kidding. That's great. I'm a little beat after driving since early this morning and was going to ask for directions to the nearest place to stay."

"Nonsense," Bart stated emphatically. "You'll stay right here tonight and get a good night's sleep. We'll both get up early tomorrow and after a good breakfast, I'll see you on your way before I report for duty."

The bond initiated three years earlier at The Citadel had now solidified since the two young military officers shared a common commitment. Although they were about to be separated by distance, they were bound as brothers devoted to their 'duty.'

Lieutenant Marks admired the Army captain and was gratified by his warm welcome and generosity. He revealed his appreciation by stating, "I'm glad I stopped by to see you, sir, and thanks for everything. You'll always be my company commander."

The reply Stan received was one that he would remember for years to come. "Never forget something, Lieutenant. Always take care of your people. There is nothing more important than that, especially now. Where we are both probably headed, things can get pretty rough. Don't ever let your people down. Always let them know that they can count on you. If you do that, when things get bad, they will be there for you as well. Don't ever let it be about you. It is and must always be about them. Okay…enough of that. How's that drink?"

He chuckled, "It's going to take some getting used to, sir, but it is getting a little better with each sip."

The two friends enjoyed another drink and reminisced over college escapades before walking back to the BOQ and retiring for the evening.

After breakfast the next morning, Bart admired Stan's new wheels and remarked about how flashy Air Force second lieutenants were. The two men had enjoyed each other's company and Stan felt honored when his old commander addressed him by his first name and asked him to do the same. As they shook hands and parted ways, the young Air Force officer reflected on the reception he received and realized that Bart was the type of man he wanted to emulate as a leader.

Stan was very much aware that half of his country disagreed with the war in Southeast Asia and although he sometimes wondered about it himself, he thought, *Why harbor doubt about your country's policies and the missions they may assign you when such leadership is, without a doubt, beyond reproach? Had such individuals not always shown us the correct path and had those paths not always taken us to greater heights for the betterment of mankind as a whole? Has this country not always been a beacon of light, providing examples for other nations and cultures to strive toward? Of course it has.*

Remember all those history courses we took during all those years of school? How could anyone think otherwise? Did we not all stand by our desks every morning, saluting our country's flag, and did we not all recite a pledge of allegiance to the flag every single day before the start of any other activity? Why, we even said a prayer immediately following that pledge. Why? Well, wasn't it because our God saw us as special people who always did good, not only for ourselves, but for others as well.

Does not every nation in the world and its people look up to us and look to us for guidance? Of course they do and they respect us for who we are. All this goes without saying...it does not need to be said. Stop trying to reason why Stan, he thought to himself.

3

As he drove south toward his destination, Lieutenant Marks decided to take a slight detour to his alma mater in Charleston, South Carolina. Last night's encounter made him realize just how much his college experiences meant to him.

As he traversed the long, old, narrow span of the Cooper River Bridge, he recalled good times with other cadets while on leave from the military college. They were cheerful, exciting times, and much needed respites from the rigors of military discipline. Rowdy cadets traditionally partied at various beach and low country locations where laughter, rough housing, and beer were always present. Those brief interludes were often all too fleeting, but went a long way in providing the renewal necessary to survive until the next great party.

As he entered the main gate to the campus, it struck him how quiet it appeared. It was July and the Corps was not present in strength or in uniform. Stan had never experienced summer sessions on campus and he was glad he had a chance to view it in a different light.

While driving past one of the main academic buildings located opposite one end of the parade ground, he realized that the last time he was there, a temporary stage had been erected across the wide expanse of stairs leading to the main entrance of the building. The stage had been built for the graduation ceremonies he had taken part in only six weeks earlier. A huge statue of an American eagle situated at the top, front, center of the structure, and the artillery pieces across the street facing the wide and long expanse of the parade ground, added to the grandeur of the event. He became thrilled with the memory of tossing his cadet garrison cap high in the air above rows of chairs placed for graduating cadets and their loved ones. The huge flutter of hundreds of white hats in the air mixed with the cheers of graduates and the smiles and laughter of all present was a sight to behold. He recalled the proud faces of his relatives, especially his parents, as he received his degree and Air Force commission.

The young Air Force second lieutenant drove around the parade ground, past the barracks where he and his cohorts had lived, dreamed, studied, marched, and sweated for four long years. That was a good portion of the life of someone who had not yet turned twenty-two years of age.

Military equipment from World War II and the Korean War was featured at each corner of the parade ground. The equipment included a tank and a jet fighter aircraft. Stan was glad that he decided to take this short detour in his journey because it revitalized his spiritual strength and resolve. He was somewhat wary and not yet sure of what lay ahead and felt himself fortified as he visualized faces and recalled voices of those he knew and had now become part of his very being.

Continuing around the parade ground, he drove past the armory, physical education, engineering, and military science buildings before turning right to complete his trip around the main part of the campus. Before reaching his exit at the main gate, he continued past the student union building, chapel, library, and museum.

He took a deep breath and a final look around before leaving the campus and thought, *Okay, let's go. Now I'm ready.*

4

The final leg of this journey was a new adventure; he was exploring unfamiliar territory. Georgia, Alabama, and Mississippi were all new to him. He devoured his new vistas as a toddler would his first taste of ice cream and now wanted to add chocolate syrup with plenty of whipped cream.

He had been well prepared by wonderful mentors to enter his chosen career field and he imagined a rewarding and exciting future. Following graduation, the majority of his former classmates were commissioned into the Army and a good many into the Air Force. He believed that he would soon be placed in positions enabling him to be of valuable assistance to brothers in arms and he wanted to perform to the best of his ability.

Lieutenant Marks wore his uniform as he drove up to the guard post at the main entrance of his training base. The AP (air policeman) on duty came to attention and saluted the young officer. The surprised expression on the policeman's face was priceless when Stan handed him a dollar bill and drove off toward the BOQ (Bachelor Officers' Quarters). As a cadet, he had been told that it was a tradition to give a dollar bill to the first person who saluted you and he laughed at the reaction of the airman on guard duty as he drove away.

The BOQ held additional surprises. Almost everyone in the building was dressed in civilian clothing and he assumed that, when off-duty, this was acceptable. The building was air conditioned and provided the best living quarters he had ever experienced. *Hey, this Air Force life is not bad,* he thought as he unpacked the few items he owned. He had been trained to live a spartan existence and considered these accommodations luxurious. After settling in, he thought, *Okay, now let's see what else is around here.* Still in uniform, Stan walked around the building and entered a lounge area equipped with sofas, tables, magazines, and lamps. The room was empty except for an attractive young lady in civilian clothing, sitting on an armchair, reading a magazine. He was planning to go to the officers' club for dinner and thought it would be nice to have some company.

The uniformed officer approached the young lady with his newly acquired air of confidence, and the conversation went something like this:

"Hi, I'm Stan. I just arrived on base and I'm headed over to the O Club (Officers' Club) for dinner. Would you care to join me?'

"Well, that does sound great, but I don't think my husband would like it very much."

"Husband? This is a bachelor officers' quarters, isn't it?"

"Yes it is. My husband is with a friend and I'm just waiting for him to get back. Thanks for asking though. It was very nice of you."

"Well, have a pleasant evening. I hope I didn't bother you."

"Not at all. Wait a minute. I have an idea if you're interested."

"Oh?"

"Yes, a friend of mine, Melanie, is attending personnel management training here and she'll be meeting us at the club later. It would be great if you could join us."

"Really?"

"Yes, she's nice and…oh, here comes my husband now. Hey Fred, meet… Sorry, what did you say your name was?" Fred was also wearing civilian clothes.

"Hello Fred, I'm Stan and I was just flirting with your pretty wife until I found out that she was married. She uh…sorry but I don't know her name either."

Fred chuckled, "It's Ann and I'll bet she is fixing you up with our friend Melanie. Right?"

"I think so. Tell me, would a wise man accept such an offer?"

"Only a very wise man. We would be happy if you would join us. Do you feel up to the challenge?" asked Fred.

"Actually, I do. What time shall I meet you?"

Ann interjected, "Melanie will meet us at the club bar for a drink before dinner at 1900 hours. See you then?"

"Yes," he said and as an afterthought added, "Thank you very much for the invitation."

Stan decided to head back to his room and freshen up before dinner at the club, since he was to meet this mysterious Air Force personnel officer named Melanie. He could not believe his good luck and felt as though he was on a real winning streak. If he knew anything about racehorses and how to bet on them, he would have wagered a good penny on one to win.

After changing into a fresh uniform, he walked to the O Club and no sooner than he entered the bar area, a bell went off. Everyone at the bar turned around and cheered, including Fred and Ann, who were still wearing civilian clothing. Stan smiled and looked at the bartender ringing the bell with an enquiring glance. The bartender pointed to a sign on the wall which said, in effect, that anyone entering the bar wearing a hat buys a round. Sure enough, he did not remove his hat prior to entering. Not wanting to break with obvious tradition and wanting to make a good first impression, he walked up to the bar area to join Fred and Ann and told the bartender to give everyone a drink. With that, everyone cheered and he gave a polite bow.

Fred said, "Hey Ann, the lieutenant knows how to make an entrance."

"Yes he does," Ann agreed.

Lieutenant Marks looked around wondering where Melanie was and noticed a tall, slim, WAF (Woman in the Air Force) approaching. She was in uniform and also held the rank of a second lieutenant. Suddenly, he was unaware of anyone else in the room. Melanie was stunning, with dark hair and captivating green eyes. As required by the military, her hair was cut short, which only served to accentuate her beauty. As she came closer, her smile seemed to say, "You need to know more about me."

Ann observed that someone captured Stan's attention. She immediately knew who it was and cheerfully exclaimed, "Oh, Melanie, glad you could make it. I'd like you to meet a new friend of ours."

Ann had a good feeling about this introduction as she said, "Stan also just arrived for training."

"Oh, for personnel training?" asked Melanie.

Still in awe of the lovely creature before him, his answer was somewhat robotic. "No, I'm here for air traffic control training."

33

Fred exclaimed, "What? I instruct that course. There are several of us, but chances are that you will be in one of my classes."

Instantly, he was brought back to the present. He now realized that he had been speaking to a superior officer. "I apologize, sir, I shouldn't have called you Fred."

Fred and Ann laughed. Fred, in a low voice, said, "Save that sir stuff for when I'm in uniform. Tonight, I'm Fred. By the way, I suggest you take care of the bar bill. You bought a round, remember? And get Melanie a drink so we can all head to dinner. I'm starving."

As always, he performed as ordered. He handed Melanie the Manhattan she requested, paid the bar bill, left a nice tip for the bartender, and escorted her, behind Fred and Ann, to a table in the next room.

During dinner, he learned that his new acquaintances had been neighbors from a small Texas town and that both Melanie and Ann were graduates of Ole Miss, The University of Mississippi. Fred was an Aggie, a Texas A&M grad. After ordering dinner, the girls excused themselves and headed to the ladies' room.

When they were out of earshot, Fred decided to provide his dinner companion with some background information. "Melanie Blake is a real lady, Stan. Her parents are both retired teachers and her father is a World War II Army veteran. Ann and I were both her parents' students at one time. She was raised with pretty strict Christian values. They are a very conservative family."

"Well, they don't come any more conservative than where I went to school. So I guess we have something in common," he remarked.

Fred motioned toward the young lieutenant's right hand as he said, "Yes, I noticed your school ring. The Citadel, right?"

Nodding affirmatively, Stan asked, "Are you familiar with the school?"

"You bet. I've run across a number of you. Why aren't you in pilot training?"

He explained that he wanted to be a flight crew member and, although physically qualified, did not pass the aptitude tests. His intention was to serve as a member of a B-52 flight crew. During his military college career, he took both written and physical examinations to measure his aptitude for flight school. He always passed the physical exams, but despite repeated attempts to enter flight training, he was turned down.

Between his third and fourth years of college, he was sent to Otis Air Force Base in Massachusetts for additional preparation prior to placement in an Air Force assignment. Asked to choose three career fields that interested him, he was given his first choice. Since he was not granted a flight school assignment, he requested air traffic control for his career field believing that was as close as he could get to an actual flying job.

"I'll bet that most of your classmates are in combat arms and that you want to do your part as well," said Fred.

The lieutenant nodded. "I hope that I am doing my part by going into air traffic control. I want to help my friends as much as possible and that's exactly what I'm trying to do."

Fred explained that he was a senior captain, a pilot, and a Vietnam veteran. He had since cross-trained to air traffic control because of injuries and was no longer able to pass the required physical exams. As Stan listened intently, Fred realized that there was something steadfast and genuine about his new acquaintance; he wanted to offer some help.

"Well, if you are still interested in flight training, I'd be more than willing to tutor you in our spare time to help you get in."

Stan's eyes widened; he couldn't believe his good fortune. "Really? If you are serious, I want to take you up on that offer!"

"Very serious," responded Fred. "There is a great need for forward air controllers today, your training here will put you way up there for such a slot after you finish flight school, and you are already on the right track. Knowledge gained here will be extremely helpful. FACs search for enemy activity, respond to requests from ground commanders, mark target areas for fighter aircraft, and lead them to the targets to support troops on the ground. I keep an eye out for people like you because we need them right now."

With that, the girls returned to the table and they had an enjoyable dinner. He took a liking to his new friends and was hoping that he would get to see more of Melanie.

Following dinner, Fred winked at Stan and said that he and Ann needed to depart early since they were no longer able to keep up with the younger folks. They all laughed and he appreciated the fact that he would get to spend a little time alone with Melanie.

Their dinner companions left the club and the smitten young man remarked, "Your friends are great, Melanie. I'm really glad they invited me tonight."

Entertaining similar thoughts, she replied, "I'm so glad you came. Ann is always trying to fix me up. She means well, but it doesn't usually turn out very well."

He gulped and said, "Well, let's hope tonight has been an exception."

Melanie found her new acquaintance to be not only handsome and well-built, but she was charmed by his serious demeanor. She stated, "Promise me you won't tell Ann, but I am really enjoying tonight."

"So am I. Let's have another drink and plan our next get together. Only next time, let's make it just the two of us."

She giggled and said, "I like the way you think."

They enjoyed a leisurely stroll toward the BOQ and after saying good night, he smiled while thinking of the coming weekend. They had planned for a nice quiet dinner in civilian clothes and off base to discuss their first week in training.

He could not believe that life was treating him so well. Just five years ago, he would never have believed this possible. His dad had been right, as usual. He always told his sons to work hard and do the very best they could because lucky people like us always make our own luck.

His grandparents had struggled to get to this country to provide their children and generations that followed with hopeful futures. He was elated that he appeared to be living up to their expectations and even surpassing his own. How could he not give his all to such a country? *People such as Fred, Ann, and Melanie appear to be accepting me as equals,* he thought. They all have long lineage in this country dating back before the Civil War. By comparison, his grandparents arrived after 1900. But that was the usual case, where he came from, and he was unable to think of a single soul he knew prior to entering college who had been able to even think about doing what he was now engaged in.

During his first week of classes, he was subjected to a great deal of technical training and no physical training at all. His studies were keeping him busy, but he knew that he needed to locate a gym on base before he started getting soft. He intended to make sure that he would always be ready for whatever physical demands were placed upon him. That ethos had been deeply engrained in him for quite some time and he was not about to become lax now since his future and the well-being of others may depend on it.

Lieutenant Marks gave more thought to what Fred told him about flight school and forward air controllers. He wrote a letter to Captain Bart Small at Fort Bragg asking him what he thought about that idea. His current training course was approximately three months long and he wanted additional input from someone he knew and trusted.

It was the summer of 1968 and another presidential election was approaching. Much had already transpired that year to cause tension and disharmony among Americans. As college students in the mid to late 1960s, Stan and Melanie had witnessed racial tension in the South, and he had also experienced similar strife in the North while on leave from his military school. Assassinations and urban riots were part of the scene and unsettling television broadcasts caused many to doubt the country's course.

Stan grew up in a Republican household. His father had been a staunch Eisenhower Republican; however, his mother did on one occasion make him promise to not ever tell Dad she had once voted for John Kennedy. He thought that was a bit humorous, especially since he admired both Eisenhower and Kennedy.

When Saturday evening arrived, he met Melanie in front of the O Club as previously arranged and she smiled broadly when she saw him drive to the entrance in his sports car. He looked at her and remembered what Fred told him, "Melanie is a real lady." He stopped his car, exited, walked to the other side, opened the door, smiled politely, bowed slightly, and said, "Your car is ready, m'lady." She smiled and, with an endearing giggle, entered his chariot.

It was a beautiful moonlit evening and the drive to a small, local restaurant overlooking a portion of the Mississippi Gulf Coast was both pleasant and relaxing. Enjoying a delicious dinner with a glass of wine in the quiet atmosphere, they were able to get to know each other a little better. Melanie seemed to be enjoying her classes, and they both laughed over silly incidents that occurred during the week.

During their conversation, he learned that Melanie was very interested in the current presidential campaign and it appeared she was a fervent supporter of Independent Party candidate George Wallace and his running mate, retired Air Force General Curtis LeMay. He listened to her thoughts, but did not offer much in return since he had not given much thought to the subject.

5

Melanie entered Ole Miss in 1964. That was just two years following the entry of James Meredith, the first black student to attend. It was a violent time on campus; federal marshals had been called in to ensure the campus would be integrated and order be restored. Two civilians were killed and many were injured, including a number of the marshals. There was still a great deal of tension, and remnants of disturbances created at the time were still evident on campus when Melanie arrived. Stan entered The Citadel in 1964 and the first black cadet to attend, Charles Foster, arrived in 1966. He was a witness to the training of that cadet and to attitudes of fellow cadets toward him. As an upperclassman, he had been impressed with the way Cadet Foster conducted himself during his arduous days and nights on campus and admired his courage. Years later, he smiled after learning Foster completed the training and did indeed graduate. *That was one tough dude,* he thought and hoped they would cross paths so he could congratulate him one day.

Stan was skeptical of most politicians, believing that he was not yet knowledgeable and experienced enough to make decisions regarding their proposed policies. He tended to listen to the advice of his father on such matters since Dad always seemed to know and he definitely had the necessary experience. He recalled phrases so often heard and so deeply engrained into the psyche of cadets at The Citadel, such as, *"In the paths our fathers showed us, follow without fear."* During his weekly Saturday evening discussions with Melanie, he conveyed to her that, as military officers, he did not believe they should overtly support political candidates. It was their duty to obey and follow the policies and orders of whatever commander in chief was in power, since he was duly elected by the American people.

That seemed to satisfy Melanie somewhat and he changed the subject telling her about Fred's offer to help him gain entry to flight school, about forward air controllers, and his interest in learning more about that career field. Her eyes widened and she said, "That sounds pretty dangerous."

"Well, I guess it all depends on what you are called upon to do. Everything in the military can be dangerous. Cooks and clerks sometimes become casualties when serving in hostile areas. When your time is up, that's it, no matter what your job."

"Yes, that's true, but why increase the odds?"

"Hmm. Well, I'm not sure what I'll be doing yet. Just trying to find out more about it, that's all. I still haven't passed the aptitude tests to enter flight training. By the way, I really like this place. It's a great little spot to relax on Saturday night. What do you think?"

"Oh yes, I really do like it here and this Manhattan is terrific."

"I bet the second one will be even better. What do you say we plan to do this every Saturday?"

"Sounds good to me, Stan. Let's do it."

And they did. They enjoyed their Saturday evening dinners and had become very close. Neither was certain they ever intended for it to become more than that. Why ruin a good thing? This was working just fine and they both found someone to bounce ideas off of, and with whom they could occasionally vent minor frustrations.

A short time after sending his letter to Bart, Lieutenant Marks received a reply. Captain Small was enthusiastic about the idea of flight school and becoming a forward air controller. He encouraged the lieutenant to pursue such training for the benefit of career progression and because he believed his friend was physically and psychologically suited for the duty. He told Stan that his type of unit benefited immensely from the services these FACs provided and that he was being trained to work with them. Bart also informed him regarding stories spread by troops returning from Vietnam. FACs had helped with the rescue of downed pilots and had come to the aid of severely outnumbered Army ground units under attack.

That did it. If Bart was so high on the idea, it was good enough for him. He wrote back to Captain Small thanking him for the input and lightheartedly stated, "Who knows, we may be working together again someday, ole friend."

He then decided to discuss this further with Fred as soon as possible.

Following a class session, he found an opportunity to approach Fred and tell him that he would like to take advantage of his tutoring offer and that he was very interested in becoming a forward air controller. Fred seemed glad to hear it and told the lieutenant to meet him at the club after classes that day to discuss it further.

While sipping the now obligatory scotch and water at the club, Fred made plans with the lieutenant to meet for one hour every day after classes to prepare for the flight school aptitude tests.

After explaining the rigors of flight training, Fred stated, "And guess where you will be headed following all of this advanced training?"

"I know, but I figured I was headed for Nam sooner or later anyway and I want to be able to provide the best service I can when I get there."

"Gotcha, I'll get the ball rolling for you right away."

"Thank you, sir, you've been a big help."

Stan began going to the gym more frequently now and he could be seen jogging around the base quite often in an attempt to get into the best possible physical condition. He intended to be ready for what lay ahead. Intensity in his classroom activity and during his after-hours study sessions with Fred became more evident. Everything seemed to be taking on a new dimension for him.

The following Saturday he again shared an evening of food and drink with Melanie at what had become their favorite little, quiet hideaway. The place seemed to be frequented by locals and they did not notice any fellow airmen from the base. If any of them were there, they were in civilian clothes and did not appear to recognize the young couple. That suited them both just fine as it gave them a nice retreat from their normal weekly activities.

At the restaurant, Stan suddenly realized he did not have the same uneasy feeling about the clientele he experienced with his brother at home prior to leaving for military service. He did not see the long hair, strange clothes, or contemptuous stares he and Pat encountered back home. New Jersey was his home he thought, or it used to be. But he now felt more at home in what had until recently been unfamiliar territory. Of course, he was in Mississippi now and in close proximity to a military installation. These were very conservative people down here, much like folks he would run across off campus at his alma mater in South Carolina. Could it be that this is where he now belonged? He looked at Melanie and smiled because it became apparent to him that he had never been in the company of a girl his age he found so appealing.

During dinner, it became evident to Melanie that Stan was excited about the possibility of attending flight school. She was happy for him but sensed his uneasiness about not passing the entry exams. They both liked each other very much, but neither really considered their relationship as anything more than friendship at this point.

Melanie asked, "Stan, do you really intend to do this?"

"I will if I am accepted into the program. Fred is arranging for me to retake the flight school exam very soon and I won't know anything more about it till I see the results. If I pass the aptitude test, of course, I'll be going to flight school and if not, I'll be assigned to a stateside base for air traffic control on-the-job training. "

She replied, "I'll be getting my first base assignment about the same time and I'm excited about that as well. You know, we could wind up just about anywhere."

"What could be more exciting than that?" He picked up his drink and nodded for her to do the same. They touched glasses and he toasted to their luck with landing great assignments.

6

Currently stationed about 90 miles from New Orleans, Stan wanted very much to experience the wonders of that enchanting city. Melanie knew the area well and entertained him with anecdotes of time spent there during her college years. Not wanting to pass up an opportunity to enjoy the city, they planned to spend time in 'The Big Easy' before leaving Biloxi.

New Orleans provided a happy diversion. They enjoyed the tourist attractions and she delighted in his fascination with what was familiar to her. He found Lake Pontchartrain, Jackson Square with its artist displays, and the paddlewheel steamship harbored along the nearby Mississippi River beyond his expectations. The entire city was like a giant amusement park with an amalgam of history, cultures, races, and traditions so unlike anything else he had ever before experienced in the Southland.

The happy couple enjoyed a carriage ride around the area and then explored places in the French Quarter such as Your Father's Mustache, Pat O'Brien's, and Al Hurt's Place. They sipped the famous hurricane drinks at Pat O'Brien's while seated at a table in an outdoor courtyard, and enjoyed the hilarity provided by sailors at two tables nearby. The sailors were also enjoying the hurricane drinks with a novel twist.

They connected straws from one table to the other and attempted to drink from the opposing table's glasses. But, they had to keep running about to keep the straw connections intact and the alcohol-fueled competition was hilarious. It was so comical watching those guys strain for all they were worth as they tried to empty the other glass first. They overheard the sailors wager and agree to pay for the winner's drinks. Unfortunately, it appeared that neither group was able to accomplish the task, but everyone else in the place seemed to thoroughly enjoy the spectacle and applauded their efforts.

They enjoyed a delicious dinner at The Top of the Mart, a rotating restaurant located at the top of a tall building with a spectacular view. Stan thought it was romantic and could see in Melanie's eyes that she must be thinking the same. His feelings for this young lady, and Fred was so right, she was indeed a lady, continued to develop. He realized that something as yet inexplicable was happening to him and that the growling he was feeling in his stomach was a result of something more than just the oysters on the half shell he had consumed earlier in the day.

Some shared experiences serve to do more than provide enjoyment and entertainment; sometimes they dwell within us, forever joining one to the other.

Both lieutenants continued with their respective studies at the base and in early October, just prior to completion of their training, they received their assignments. After a short leave back home in New Jersey, Lieutenant Marks was ordered to report to Laughlin Air Force Base, Del Rio, Texas for flight school training.

Saturday date night with Melanie was approaching and although he was excited about the good news, he was also a little apprehensive. Nothing could dampen his enthusiasm more than not being able to continue seeing her. At this point, he was anxious to hear where she would be stationed.

Well, they were at their preferred table, in their much-loved restaurant, with their favorite waitress, Emma. The young couple had become well known to the establishment by this time and were now treated as special guests. Melanie and Stan were both beaming. They were obviously happy with their new assignments and couldn't wait to tell each other.

The waitress sensed that this was a special occasion and told the owner, Jack, that something was up. The owner had taken a liking to these two kids; they were always friendly and respectful. He told Emma to let them know their drinks were on the house tonight. They both waved to Jack, thanking him.

"Okay, Stan," she said. "So where are you going to flight school?"

"Did Fred tell you that? How did you know I made it?"

"Are you kidding, it's written all over your face."

"I guess I am a bit up in the clouds. I'm going somewhere else I've never been, but that covers a lot of territory. Laughlin Air Force Base, Del Rio, Texas. So what am I in for Texas girl?"

"Well, hope you like jack rabbits and tumbleweed. Cause you're headed for wide open country Jersey boy."

"Hmm...I'll be there for a year, but from what I hear, I won't have much time to become acquainted with either rabbits or weeds. So, where is the prettiest soldier I know headed?"

Melanie beamed at that remark and stated that she was headed for Cannon Air Force Base, near Clovis, New Mexico.

"By the look on your face, I take it that's good news?"

"Very good news. I could drive to my parents' home in Texas, if I want to, whenever I have some time off, and I will

47

be staying there for a week on leave before going to Cannon Air Force Base. How about you, are you taking leave?"

"Yes, I'm also taking a week. Guess I'll go home to Jersey before heading to Laughlin."

"Wow, that's an awful lot in a week! Mississippi to New Jersey and then to Texas all in a week by car?"

"Well, I guess I could fly to Jersey for a couple of days and then fly back here to get my car before heading off to Texas. Crazy, huh?"

"You bet it's crazy. I've got a better idea. My parents' place is in Abilene. It's on your way to Del Rio. Come stay at our place on your leave and then go on to flight school."

The startled lad's eyes widened and he developed a mischievous smile comparable only to the one worn by Melanie.

"Wow. That would be great, Melanie. But how would your parents feel about that?"

"Oh, I've told them all about you. Did you know that you're the greatest thing since horseshoes?"

With a big smile, he said, "No, I didn't, but I guess they do come in handy in Texas. At least they did for John Wayne and his buddies. We watch a lot of TV in Jersey. But seriously, stay in your parents' home for a week?"

"No trouble at all. I didn't tell you that my parents are retired teachers. They love to travel and will be away that week. Oh, and I'm an only child."

He was surprised; his mouth was slightly open, and his eyes were getting wider and wider. She began to laugh and said, "Big cowboy afraid of little ole me?"

"Uh, maybe a little. This sounds too good to be true. Are you sure about this?"

"I've had some time to think about it. You see, there are a lot of pilot training bases in Texas and I thought this might happen. Abilene is a nice quiet town and I'd love to show you around. Interested?"

"Won't your neighbors talk?"

"Neighbors? We live on the outskirts of town and you'll need binoculars to see one. Besides, we don't worry about those things back home. We tend to mind our own business where I come from."

"Hmm, if I turn this down, I'll kick myself for the rest of my life."

"If you turn this down, I'll kick you right now."

He laughed and said, "You know, Fred and Ann did a lot for us and me especially. What do you say we take them out for a nice dinner before we go?"

"I like that. Yes, let's do it."

They made the arrangements, and Fred and Ann met them at the quiet, little hideaway restaurant they frequented.

"How did you two ever find this place?" asked Ann. "I love it here. The view is nice and it's so cozy."

"The food is great and the staff is very friendly," added Melanie.

Stan said, "We are very lucky, especially me. Not only for finding this place, but also for finding each other. Hey, Fred, uh sorry, Sir Fred that is, turns out that flirting with your wife was one of the best things I ever did."

"What?" said Melanie as Fred and Ann laughed.

"Sure, if I hadn't noticed that pretty person sitting by herself in the BOQ lounge, I may never have met you and Fred."

"We are glad you did, Stan," said Ann. "As soon as you spoke to me, I thought about Melanie and how I needed to introduce you."

"Thank you for that," he replied. "And Fred, thank you so much for all your help. I never fully realized how disappointed I was about not getting into flight school before. I just did my best to accept it and you changed all that. Thanks."

"You bet, Stan. Happy to have been of some help and I just know you will do well."

"Okay, now it's my turn," said Melanie. "Will you two promise to stop trying to fix me up?"

Ann and Fred thought that was humorous, and Ann said, "It appears that will no longer be necessary, Melanie."

7

The distance from Biloxi, Mississippi to Abilene, Texas is approximately 750 miles. They left at 0500 hours and stopped only for fuel and a midday meal. Stan followed Melanie's Volkswagen Bug in his Firebird. Neither car had much interior room or trunk space; however, both had more than enough room for all of their personal belongings. *There are certain benefits to having few possessions,* he thought, and he enjoyed believing that he now had a companion to share his carefree existence. If he could change anything at all, it would be having Melanie on the passenger seat next to him. There were so many things that were new to him as they traveled through country well known to her, but totally unfamiliar to him. He wanted to ask her questions and hoped they would not slip his mind when he had a chance to ask.

As a former student and a graduate of the University of Mississippi, Melanie was very familiar with the route she was now taking with Stan to her home in Texas. She was so happy that he agreed to stay with her at her parents' home and was hoping that he would not be disappointed. Melanie had developed deep feelings for him and wanted very much to be a part of his life. He was not like the boys she was used to dating. Always cheerful and kind, he reminded her very much of her father, whom she loved dearly. The boys she knew prior to meeting Stan were…well, they were boys. They did not seem to be serious about much of anything worthwhile. She believed that her new boyfriend was conscientious and honorable; it appeared that he wanted to do something of value. Melanie wanted to be with him and wanted so much for him to enjoy being with her in the home she loved in Abilene.

She smiled to herself while thinking of his expression when she offered to let him stay with her, and how her own behavior had been so out of character. Was she trying to seduce Stan? What did he think about all of this? She was a little afraid of herself at this point, but she was ready to just let things happen. Why? Because she not only trusted him, but because she wanted very much to be with him.

The duo was quite a sight traveling across open roadway between Biloxi, Mississippi and Abilene, Texas. The candy apple red Pontiac Firebird with black racing stripes following the baby blue Volkswagen Beetle was akin to Popeye chasing Olive Oyl across a lake on row boats. The sight could make one wonder when she might decide to turn her boat around and catch him.

Stan was grateful that Melanie was not a speed demon since his red hot wheels with New Jersey license plates could be a very tempting target for law enforcement officers in The Deep South. He was familiar with such circumstances from his cadet days in South Carolina. Although he did not own a car as a cadet, he did have occasion to drive cars owned by other cadets bearing New York and Massachusetts license plates, and his affiliation with the military college saved him more than once.

They arrived at the Blakes' family home at about 1800 hours. He was enthralled. This was something out of his boyhood dreams. A long dirt road from a local paved roadway meandered for a good distance before reaching the home site. The house was a well-kept, older, ranch style home with a large covered front porch that extended the entire length of the structure. There were no other houses that could be seen, not even with binoculars. He half expected to see the Cartwright family show up on horseback and Ben announcing that Hop-Sing had just finished preparing a scrumptious dinner for the newly arrived, weary travelers.

After Melanie exited her Bug, Stan looked at her and said, "Geez, I think my entire hometown of thousands would easily fit on this homestead. How big is this place?"

"Not very big really," said Melanie. "It's only five hundred acres."

"Oh, pardon me, only five hundred acres."

"Come inside. I'll show you around."

"Melanie, is that a barn way out there?"

"Yes it is, and we keep a few horses back there. Do you ride?"

"I was on a pony once when I was about three years old back in 1949. The only reason I know that is because my parents had a picture of me on what I think was a Shetland pony. It was taken in New Jersey, where my grandparents lived. A local guy named Danny gave pony rides to kids while he held the reins and walked along the street."

She chuckled and said, "Well, while you're here, we'll see if we can remedy that neglected part of your education."

They walked up to the front door of the house and Melanie opened it without a key. "Hey, someone is here," said Stan.

"Where?" she asked.

"The door wasn't locked. You just opened it."

"This door has never been locked. That would be such a nuisance, who wants to keep track of all those keys?"

"I see," he remarked with amazement.

They entered the house and the first thing he noticed was a huge stone fireplace set in a rustic, yet tastefully decorated living room. It was obvious that an outdoorsman with a penchant for hunting and fishing was a resident. Paintings and wall-mounted décor indicated a love of nature and its offerings. The interior of the home was more spacious than it appeared during the drive toward its entrance, and the kitchen adjoining a dining and entertaining area looked like a chef's dream. He looked around in awe, and said, "I just love this place. Thank you so much for inviting me. This is great."

"Do you really like it?"

"You bet I do. This kitchen is amazing. Someone must like cooking."

"Yes, and let's have something to eat. My mom is a great cook and she always has some good leftovers in the fridge."

After a nice meal, they sat in a long, comfortable, wicker chair on the front porch with a glass of wine. It was October and the weather was pleasant. Stan was impressed with how quiet and peaceful it was. This was so different from anything he had ever experienced. He was used to noise, hustle and bustle, loud people, and fast talk. *Wow, everything about me is changing,* he thought, *and I think I like the change.*

"Melanie, what was it like growing up here?"

"My folks always kept me busy. Outdoor activities are big here, as you might imagine. Horseback riding, swimming, fishing, boating, hunting, all that sort of thing. Sports are big among the guys and I was a cheerleader in high school. Mom and Dad spent their entire lives here, and they did their best to make sure I studied hard and tried to do something useful with my life."

"Well, I know you studied hard or you wouldn't be where you are. So, what is it that you want to do with your life?"

"I'm still not sure, but I know I want you to be a part of it, and I hope you feel the same way."

Melanie's words in that unguarded statement were just what he needed to hear. His feelings for this beautiful, spirited girl had grown immensely. At that moment, he realized he could no longer imagine his life without her.

"You became a part of my life from the moment we met. I know we'll be stationed far from each other, but I want to see you as often as possible."

It was obvious that Melanie had already come up with a plan, and she laid it out excitedly. "Well, we can meet here in Abilene when we can arrange time off together, and it won't really take that long for either of us to get here. As you can see, there is plenty of room for you in this house, and I would love for my folks to meet you."

Stan had been concerned about what the future held for them if their lives went in separate directions. Suddenly, the future was looking very bright.

"I accept with pleasure and let's hope we can make that happen often."

Melanie was proud of her hometown and couldn't wait to show her boyfriend around. Abilene has a frontier history which still appealed to the little boy dwelling within him. He grew up watching western movies and he found all of this stirring. This is where cattle ranchers, U.S. Cavalry, forts, cattle trails, cowboys, Indians, and the whole bit actually took place. She took him to a museum with artifacts that he was thrilled to see, and she was so happy to bring out the young boy in Stan, the boy she wished she had known growing up.

They strolled along a main thoroughfare toward a small café for a light lunch when someone exclaimed in a loud voice, "Hey Melanie, that you, ole girl? How the hell you been?" They turned toward the voice and two young men, about their age, approached.

Stan was a little taken aback by their demeanor as they sauntered toward them, but Melanie immediately engaged them in conversation. She introduced him to the pair and about all he managed to say was hello when they turned their attention back to Melanie. One of them didn't say much, but she acknowledged his presence. The talkative one had an awful lot to say and Stan gathered that they were old high school friends. Being ignored was not much fun and after a while, he began to feel like a motorcycle sidecar. It was just there waiting for someone to sit on it.

He started to gaze around the local area, taking in the sights, since he did not feel included. Melanie seemed to sense his uneasiness and, while still very much involved in conversation, moved her left hand over and clasped his right hand. Stan welcomed this affirmation of their affection. He simply squeezed her hand gently and she responded in kind. The pair of young men finally seemed to get the message as Melanie politely bid them a nice day and Stan exchanged nods with them before heading into the cafe.

"Nice to see old friends, isn't it, Melanie?"

"Well, sometimes it's nice to leave old friends too," she said with a knowing smile.

Two
Aim

1

Lieutenant Marks immediately began to realize that he had a
leg up on his classmates in flight school. During air traffic
control training, he learned about control tower and radar
approach control procedures. He also learned about weather,
navigational aids, radio procedures, emergency procedures,
aircraft characteristics, and a host of other variables as yet
unfamiliar to many of his new counterparts. As a result, he
started to become helpful to his new friends and instructors.
He was also happy to discover that one of his old college
classmates, Eric Summers, was now joining him in flight
training.

Stan started his military career almost immediately after
college graduation, while others were not scheduled to report
for duty until slots became available months later. As a result,
he did not lose any time and gained valuable knowledge.

Initial flight instruction was conducted in single engine
propeller driven Cessna aircraft and that training took place off
base at the Del Rio Airport. The aircraft was a Cessna 172 or
a T-41 Mescalero in Air Force parlance. He loved the aircraft
and took to it like Popeye to spinach. The budding pilot liked
to fly low and slow over the landscape that seemed to never
end. Putting his aircraft through maneuvers was even more

enjoyable than the horseback riding lessons given to him by Melanie a short time ago.

Stan did not take to riding a horse that easily. He found it uncomfortable perched upon such a large creature so high above the ground and he laughed while thinking about his first ride. The greenhorn equestrian would not remove his hands from the saddle horn and he bounced up and down so much his sunglasses began to slip from his nose. Putting them back in place was difficult since he was fearful of removing his hands from the horn long enough to adjust them. Melanie had been riding a horse ahead of him and he didn't want her to notice he was anxious. The sunglasses finally fell to the ground and he never said a word about it.

Unlike riding a horse, he felt very comfortable in his Cessna and began to feel as one with the machine, much as he felt about driving his Firebird. Both Stan and Eric, his old classmate from college, progressed well in their initial phase of training and they looked forward to the next step. That would be back at the base flying T-37 jet aircraft.

It took about four hours for Stan to drive from Abilene to Del Rio and about the same time for Melanie to drive from her home to Clovis. They communicated by letter and made plans when both were able to meet again at the Blake Ranch. He met Melanie's parents during his visits and they prepared a guestroom for his stay. He began to feel like part of the family and enjoyed spending time with her father. Her dad was a real character who liked telling his visitor old stories about military service in the Philippines during the war. He loved to laugh and he enjoyed teaching Stan some of the finer points of horseback riding, which was becoming more enjoyable. His daughter was happy about the growing relationship and as she watched it develop, it seemed to her that her boyfriend was quickly becoming the son her father never had. They were so much alike and a partnership seemed to be brewing.

One day Mr. Blake said to Stan, "Do these belong to you by any chance?" as he retrieved a pair of Air Force aviator sunglasses from his pocket.

Sheepishly and after clearing his throat, he replied, "Well, yes sir, I believe they do. You see, the first time I rode one of your horses, I bounced around quite a bit. But that's okay, you see I did pretty much the same thing the first time I tried to fly an airplane down in Del Rio."

They laughed together and he made a gift of the sunglasses to Mr. Blake saying, "I'd very much like you to have them, sir. You see, they gave me another pair back at the base."

Stan wished he could do more to repay the kindness shown to him by the Blake family and decided to offer his services at whatever chores needed to be accomplished during his visits. Mr. Blake appreciated the offer and decided to show his new young friend an area in the barn used as a workshop. Stan was intrigued with some of the items, and they had a great time tinkering with some unusual old tools. Melanie's dad seemed to take great pleasure in teaching him how to use and maintain the equipment stored there. Some of the implements stored in the barn appeared to be antiques indicating that the family had quite a history at the ranch.

Mr. Blake's new friend and occasional ranch hand also took an interest in the horses kept there and learned a great deal about how to care for them. Stan looked forward to spending time with his new mentor while Melanie was busy in the house with her mother. This work was more like a hobby to him; it had actually become downtime and it helped rest his mind after a week or so of studies and flight training at the base. Mr. Blake was knowledgeable in areas unfamiliar to him and he thought that Melanie's dad must have been a great high school teacher because of his patience; he was so kind and mild mannered in his approach to teaching.

Now, Melanie's mother was another story. She was a great cook. While in the kitchen, which seemed to be always, the aromas throughout the entire house made mouths water. She was a natural at making people feel comfortable in her home and Stan was a definite beneficiary of that virtue. Mrs. Blake took note of the food he enjoyed and did her utmost to have mouth-watering delicacies on hand during his visits. He loved her fresh baked pies and the variety she served seemed endless.

"I really like Stan and so does your father," Mrs. Blake said to her daughter when they were alone. "And in case you haven't noticed, I think he really cares about you."

"Oh Mom, I hope so 'cause I really think he's special."

"So, what are you waiting for? When are you going to make me a grandma?"

"MOM, STOP IT! Not for at least another nine months."

"WHAT?"

Melanie roared with laughter at her mother's reaction and they both enjoyed the moment.

Stan saw that Melanie had a great relationship with her parents, especially her mom. Mrs. Blake was intelligent, kind, and considerate. She was also quite attractive, and he believed that she must have once been as beautiful as her daughter. He could now see why Fred and Ann were proud to have been students of the Blakes and why they took such an interest in Melanie. Melanie was an awful lot like her mom and he thought that was certainly a very good thing.

2

The T-37 Air Force trainer aircraft was affectionately known as Tweety Bird. With engines running, it has a very loud whining or shrieking sound, especially while taxiing. It has two turbo jet engines and sits low to the ground due to its short landing gear. That permits easy access to the cockpit without the help of a ladder. The aircraft has a side-by-side cockpit, allowing instructors to monitor students closely, and gives students the ability to observe the actions of instructors. The cockpit has a clamshell-like canopy hinged at its rear that opens upward. The student pilots would now be flying faster and at higher altitudes than in their previous aircraft, but not as high or as fast as they will during the final phase of pilot training.

Stan and Eric were now able to live off base during this phase of training and they rented a small house in Del Rio. They worked well together, compared notes, swapped stories, and helped each other with their studies.

Eric was from Florida and was an avid water skier. Stan had never been on water skis before, but Eric wanted to share the cost of buying a small motorboat powerful enough to tow water skiers at nearby Lake Amistad. That sounded great to Stan and he looked forward to getting boating and water ski lessons from his good friend. They decided to go for it and purchased a boat they believed could be sold to pilots in training classes behind them following their graduation.

Eric was a free spirit and was usually up for anything exciting. He did a lot to make life interesting and relieve some of the stress from constant study and training. That daredevil was always attempting different maneuvers on water skis and would get Stan to try as well. One day Eric showed up with an old motorcycle he bought from an airman on base who had been transferred to a remote location. His roommate took one look at the new toy and said, "Damn, now I have to live with Evil Knievel. Hey, Eric, you aren't going to try to fly that damn thing now, are you?"

"Hell, you bet I am, Pollock. Hop on the back, boy. We're goin' for a ride."

"Well, I'll be damned," said Stan as he hopped on the back behind Eric and off they went having a good ole time.

Good grief, he thought. *What will I be learning next? Air traffic control, aircraft piloting, horseback riding, and now water skiing, and boating. It really wasn't that long ago that I first learned to drive a car. Hell, make hay while the sun shines, I guess, but do I really want to learn how to ride a motorcycle?*

It wasn't very long before he found out what it was that he would be learning next though. He received a letter from Melanie saying that on his next visit, her father wanted to take him turkey hunting. *Hunting? For turkey? Always thought those suckers came from butcher shops and restaurants,* he laughed. *Okay, I'm up for this as well. Firearm training is something I may need, and what better person to learn from than an Army infantry veteran.* He had spent hours cleaning, disassembling, reassembling, practicing manual of arms, and marching with an M-1 rifle at The Citadel for four years, but that was about the extent of his training in that area. The school was well known for its high quality rifle team, but he had never been involved in that endeavor.

While sharing lunch together at the base bowling alley snack area, the two pilot trainees noticed a familiar face at the lunch counter. "Hey Stan, isn't that Rich from A Company?" The military college they attended had an Army-style organization. The entire Corps comprised a regiment of approximately 2,000 cadets divided into four battalions. Each battalion was housed in its own square-shaped building containing an open courtyard at its center utilized for formations prior to drills, parades, physical training, and various other activities. 'A' Company was located in the first battalion barracks area.

"I think you're right," said Stan and he yelled over to the counter, "Hey Rich, I see you over there. Quit hiding from us and get your butt over here, boy."

Rich turned around with a smile on his face, having recognized a familiar irreverent voice. As he approached their table, he said "God damn. It's that big Yankee Pollock. What the hell you doing here, boy?"

"Just about to ask you the same friggin' question."

Lieutenant Marks was amazed at how many classmates from college he had already encountered during his short military career. But then just about every graduate took a commission in one branch or another of the service. A military draft was in effect at that time and not accepting a commission meant almost certain induction into the Army as a private. After four years of military training, few chose that option.

Almost everyone he knew supported the war in Southeast Asia. It was considered unpatriotic by his associates to even question decisions made by our governmental leaders. At that time, it did not even enter his mind or the minds of any of his cohorts, as far as he knew, to think about why so many students in civilian colleges and universities across the country vehemently opposed the war.

Was it unpatriotic to oppose military actions taken by your country's government when you believed it was wrong or was it unpatriotic to go along with those actions when you thought it may be wrong because you were afraid of being labeled unpatriotic? Those were not questions he had ever thought about. There were far too many other things occupying his young mind. Even if someone had brought up the subject, and it never was, the old adage would have probably held true. You can always tell a second lieutenant, you just can't tell him very much. At least not about certain things, that is.

Many of Stan's high school classmates who did not attend college had been drafted while he was enrolled at the military school. Some of them had already been killed, some wounded, and others suffered psychological impairments and physical damage of which they were not yet aware. For better or worse, he lost contact with those individuals and never did benefit from exposure to their knowledge and experience.

Stan welcomed Rich to join them for lunch and said, "You remember Eric from T Company, right?"

"Oh, yeah, how the hell are you? I remember you. We never talked much but we walked punishment tours for hours together on the number two barracks quadrangle. That was you, wasn't it?"

Punishment tours were awarded to cadets for accumulating too many demerits during a given period of time or for other infractions looked down upon by the chain of command.

"Yeah, that was me and I do remember you now. What do you do here, Rich?"

"I'm a watch supervisor at the radar approach control facility, the RAPCON located between the parallel runways on base."

"What?" exclaimed Stan. "When were you at Keesler?"

"Got there in August following graduation. You know about Keesler?"

"Yeah, I was in the class just ahead of you. We were there at the same time and didn't know it. After finishing up there, I got into flight school. Eric and I are in the same class."

"Well, I'll be damned. I don't ever see you guys at the BOQ. Where are you staying?"

"We're renting a house in town," said Stan. "Hey Eric, we sure could use a third guy to share expenses considering the boat and all."

"Hell yeah," said Eric. "C'mon Rich, join us. Cid grads need to be together and we've all got a lot to catch up on."

Cid grads was a reference to graduates of The Citadel, their shared alma mater.

"You guys have a boat?"

"Yeah, time off at Lake Amistad is great and a third guy on the boat is really a good idea when water skiing. What do you say?"

"Damn, today is my lucky day. Count me in."

3

The addition of Rich to the group proved to be of valuable assistance to both Stan and Eric. His knowledge of local air traffic procedures as well as equipment available to them made life somewhat easier and more interesting. Rich, the air traffic control officer, gave them both tours of the control tower, RAPCON and GCA (Ground Control Approach) facilities. He introduced them to the air traffic controllers on duty and that aided in establishing a camaraderie within the local aviation community.

The three roommates got a kick out of practicing pilot/controller phraseology together with Stan and Eric acting as pilots and Rich, of course, as controller. They acted out various scenarios and more often than not came up with humorous variations to actual procedure.

The two pilots thought it might be a good idea to rent a Cessna at Del Rio Airport and take their air traffic control roommate on a local area flight so he could gain greater perspective from a pilot's point of view. Rich loved the idea and made arrangements with controllers on duty during a weekend. He let them know that he and his flying buddies would be showing up to practice low approaches at the air base. It worked out so well that he decided to try expanding the operation with his liaison officer at the flying school and arrange training flights for air traffic control personnel in his unit.

T-37 flight training was progressing very well for both potential pilots and they were starting to get a little cocky. Rich noticed that their pilot/controller phraseology was getting a little salty. Runway Supervisory Units (RSUs) were located near the runways and not too far from the RAPCON supervised by Rich. The RSUs were staffed by instructor pilots who were in contact with students doing pattern work to runways controlled by their respective RSU.

There were three parallel runways at the base and the two outside runway operations were generally operated by flight instructors in the RSUs while the center runway by the control tower. The RSUs were called Honcho and Lariat, the first for T-37 and the other for T-38 operations respectively. Rich became familiar with some of the RSU controllers and during a routine visit one day knew that both Stan and Eric were in the same pattern at that time.

After listening to the operation for a short time, he recognized his roommates' voices and picked up their call signs. Rich looked at the supervisor on duty and asked for permission to make a short transmission. The request was a very unusual one, but Rich was an air traffic control supervisor and he did advise that both of his pals were in the pattern. The RSU supervisor looked at Rich and told him to make this very short as he handed him the mike. Using their call signs, Rich gruffly said, "Clean up that phraseology you bums or you are both confined to barracks this weekend." He then handed the mike back to the smiling, laughing, and backslapping supervisor.

Stan and Eric were both startled and it took them a while to realize what had just happened. After landing and debriefing, they compared notes and wondered why in God's name was Rich in that RSU. They recognized his voice and knew exactly what Rich was referring to. The "you bums and confinement to barracks" quotes were taken from a well-known and highly respected assistant Commandant of Cadets at The Citadel. That transmission had to come from someone they knew intimately.

Later that evening, while the two pilot trainees were drinking some beer in their quarters off base, Rich returned from his shift and looked at his roommates with a sly smirk on his face. His roommates looked annoyed and Eric said, "What the hell is the big idea?" Rich suddenly looked concerned and said, "Hey, you guys. Yeah, both of you. You are both getting sloppy with your phraseology and I'm worried that it may in part be my fault."

"Is that supposed to be an excuse?" asked Stan.

"No, it is not. It is meant to be a statement. Sloppiness in such an obvious area tends to make me believe that you may be getting sloppy in other areas as well. What you guys are engaged in is very serious business and I am trying to hit you both over your heads hard enough to make you understand that. I want to be proud of my pilot buddies and I'll be damned if I'll be attending any of your funerals. Have I made myself clear?"

His pilot buddies looked at each other and appeared very thoughtful. Neither of them said a word until Stan finally mumbled under his breath, "Hey Eric, get Rich a beer."

4

Stan had been thinking about Melanie a lot lately and wanted to begin planning their future together. However, he still had so much training ahead of him. He wondered if he really had much to offer. I'm a soldier and I'm probably heading to a war zone. Stability is something he thought women wanted and deserved. But Melanie was an Air Force officer; she knew the game and she hadn't come close to chasing him off yet.

Her father, Jeff Blake, took great pains in teaching the basics of firearm safety to Stan before they headed off to a ranch about thirty miles from Abilene to hunt wild turkey. During the trip, he talked about what to expect and how to take proper precautions. As a budding aviator, Stan was becoming very familiar with the necessity of following procedure. He knew that safety was always of paramount importance not only for him, but for all others he encountered while engaged in any hazardous activity, and Mr. Blake appreciated his attentiveness to instructions.

The outing proved both enjoyable and successful. They spent the day together and the bond they had forged became even stronger. During the return trip, the conversation shifted to a more personal level. Mr. Blake indicated that he and his wife had grown very fond of him and they liked seeing their daughter so happy.

These words were music to his ears; he had developed a great affection for this wonderful family. But he confided that as much as he might want to, he was reluctant to make any long-term commitments at this time because his future was so uncertain.

As the conversation progressed, the older man sensed a deep-rooted integrity in the young lieutenant and, as a result, felt comfortable explaining that he understood exactly how he felt. Jeff Blake had been in the Army when he married his wife. They were wed just before his overseas deployment and he received news that he was going to be a father while he was in the Philippines.

"That must have been pretty tough on both of you," Stan said.

"It was tough any way you look at it. But under such circumstances, we felt that it was much better to have had even a short time together than to have never been together at all."

"Hmm. Thanks for that. I wonder how Melanie feels about it."

"Only one way to find out, Stan. What you decide is between you, but Mrs. Blake and I are happy that you have become a part of our lives."

They each had a bird to bring back to the ladies and when they returned, he had the pleasure of learning how to clean and prepare the turkeys before bringing them into the house.

After dinner that evening, he was alone with Mr. Blake in the living room while Melanie and her mom were clearing the dishes. They were enjoying a drink together as they rehashed their hunting adventure.

After a while, Stan remarked, "It's nice outside tonight and I'd like a little time alone with Melanie on the porch if that's alright?"

"You bet it's alright. I'll see that you get all the time you need."

"Thank you, sir."

Mr. Blake excused himself and entered the kitchen with his wife and daughter. A short time later, Melanie emerged from the house and said, "Dad told me to keep you company and that he would help Mom with the dishes." She had a confused look on her face and purred in a low voice, "Dad help with the dishes? Everything okay? Is something wrong?"

"No, nothing at all. I just asked him for some time alone with you on the porch. I'll be heading back to base in the morning and I want to talk to you."

It was a nice spring evening and sipping wine while sitting on the front porch in such an idyllic setting made him feel as though he was starring in one of those old romantic movies where he was courting his favorite girl and about to stammer through an awkward heartfelt moment. *Damn it,* he thought, *this is a heartfelt moment. Stutter, stammer, make a damn fool of yourself and do what you want to do. Just do it.*

"Melanie, I've been thinking and I'm not sure you are going to like this idea, so tell me what you think. Okay?"

"Okay."

"Well, we've been seeing each other for quite some time now and well...well, I don't want it to end."

"Why should it end?"

"Huh, it...it shouldn't."

"Stan, what has gotten into you?"

"Well, I think I'd like us to be more of a couple and I don't want to mess this up, Melanie. You see, I love you...and I want to marry you...and I didn't plan this out properly,...and I feel like a first class jerk,...and I don't even have a ring with me and, damn it,...I feel like a cheap Jimmy Stewart imitation.

Will you marry me? I'll get you a ring as soon as I can get you to the right store and we can find you one that you like and that I can afford. Boy, I am a big jerk."

With a joyful smile, Melanie said, "Well, if this is a proposal, you big jerk, yes, I will marry you!"

"Huh, you will? Even after that horrible proposal?"

"Especially because of that wonderful proposal. I love you too and don't worry about the ring right now, and we will take our time about setting a wedding date. Okay?"

"You know what, Melanie?"

"What?"

"I think we just did a good thing."

"I love you," they both said, and that said it all.

5

Eric and Stan finally successfully completed their T-37 training and were now preparing to enter the final phase of flight school in T-38s. The aircraft, a beautiful flying machine, is called a Talon or a "white rocket" by some. It is a high altitude, supersonic jet aircraft with swept wings, tricycle landing gear, and a steerable nose wheel. It has a tandem cockpit where unlike the T-37, the student and instructor sit one behind the other. This was a glamorous phase of training where every student had his photograph taken holding his flight helmet while posing during entrance into the cockpit. That photograph is proudly displayed as part of many family galleries, and these new pilots were looking forward to that photo day. Many family members, including wives and girlfriends would be receiving them.

Stan had recently received a letter from his old friend, Army Captain Bart Small. Bart's unit was being deployed shortly to Vietnam and he inquired as to his friend's progress in flight school. He had mixed feelings while thinking about what he read and didn't know whether to feel happy or sad for Bart. He knew that Bart was a great leader and a career Army officer; he was where he wanted to be and doing what he wanted to do. Captain Small had prepared himself for this so-called opportunity for many years just as he and so many others had.

Something deep within the young lieutenant was nagging him. While it nagged him and nagged him, he also suppressed it and suppressed it. *What were we doing over there? Stan knew why he was going. He was going because he wanted to help his friends who were being sent to Vietnam and those who would soon be going there. But why were his friends serving in such a far-flung region in the first place? They went because our country ordered them to go and they went believing it was their patriotic duty, but why was our country sending them?*

Lieutenant Marks was taught and he believed that we were in that country protecting South Vietnamese and Americans from communist domination. He had been told that we were there to protect the South Vietnamese from takeover by an oppressive regime.

He had more questions: *Was this worth the cost in American lives and fortune? This venture was obviously tearing his beloved country apart and how were the South Vietnamese viewing these American sacrifices and so-called good deeds?*

Once again, Lieutenant Marks put his doubts aside. He was an American Air Force officer and it was his sworn duty to obey orders. Many of his friends were in harm's way and it was his duty to help protect and aid them in the performance of their duty. He then thought of an inscription written on a plaque plainly visible to him and read by him almost daily as a cadet. It read, *"Duty is the sublimest word in the English language."* Those words were purportedly spoken by General Robert E. Lee. The plaques were hung in the main sally port of barracks on The Citadel campus. *End of discussion boy,* he thought to himself. He then sat down and drafted a reply to

Bart's letter. The note advised him of his progress, wished Bart well in his new assignment, and told him of his relationship with Melanie. He also wrote about rooming with two fellow grads.

Lieutenant Marks was now a pilot, an air traffic controller, a horseback rider, a hunter, a water skier, a boating enthusiast, and soon to be a husband. But he was still not sure about this damn motorcycle stuff. *Well anyway, if the folks back home could only see me now,* he thought.

He suddenly realized that his family, including his brother Pat, knew little about what he had been doing. Stan had received a few letters and he did reply to them, but that correspondence told him little more than everything was okay and that Pat would be entering his final year at The Citadel in the fall. He believed it might be time to let them know there was a person in his life named Melanie but he didn't want to tell them much more just yet. As a family member, he decided it was probably time to say just enough to keep them from being totally surprised.

Another letter needed to be written. This one was for Melanie. He wanted to meet her next weekend in Abilene to take her and her parents out to dinner. Stan wished to express his gratitude to them for being so kind and generous for so long. However, he did not inform her of his intention to officially ask her to marry him during that dinner and present her with an engagement ring. She already said yes and he was not concerned about asking again in front of her parents. He also suspected that they were aware of what was happening. He read what he had just written and said to himself, "Fred told me that only a very wise man would take on this challenge. Stan ole boy, you are a very wise man."

6

The T-38 is a hot, fun-filled, thrill machine. It can also be intimidating and somewhat daunting to the novice. Stan equated this new challenge to that of learning to ride a horse and learning to water ski. The pilot trainee had an advantage this time; he had already learned to fly T-41s and T-37s. There was also an instructor pilot on board the aircraft until he was ready to go solo. The lieutenant had been alone while on horseback and water skis. If he could meet those challenges head on, there was no reason why this should be any different.

After hours of training with instructors, Stan and Eric were finally ready for solo flights and pattern work under the observation and control of the RSU designated for T-38s. Once released from pattern training, they began to practice maneuvers in training areas assigned specifically for their use. The base is located just north of the Rio Grande River and Mexico. They were supposed to remain clear of Mexican airspace and remain within the confines of their practice areas while conducting maneuvers. But they were students and, of course, the idea is to let them make errors, point out those errors, and have them continue training until they master control and are fully able to utilize the characteristics of the machine. Well, student pilot training squadrons designed patches for their individual units and there was a reason why

Stan and Eric's patches read '100 Missions over North Mexico.'

While off-duty, Stan spent some time browsing through a jewelry store in Del Rio looking for an engagement ring. He wanted the ring to be something Melanie would really like, as well as a reflection of her personality. Something elegant and sophisticated would be perfect – just like her. It was a tall order for him since he did not know the first thing about jewelry.

During his third trip to the same store, he approached the young sales girl he had met during his first two trips and said, "Okay, this is how much I have to spend on an engagement ring." As he placed his available cash on the counter, he questioned the wisdom of his actions but decided to continue.

He then said, "Which ring would you want to receive if the ring were to be yours?"

The girl laughed and said, "Is this a proposal?"

Stan broke a smile and said, "Sorry, but I've already done that elsewhere. Can you help me? I'm a bit confused."

And help she did. "I know what I would like. Let me get it for you," she said as she moved toward another end of the counter. The sales girl removed a ring from beneath the counter, placed it on her finger, and told him, "This is the ring I hope to get someday." The band was yellow gold with a glittering pear-shaped diamond set high in the center. It was elegant and sophisticated; it was perfect.

He could picture the ring on Melanie's finger. The sales girl was built similar to his fiancé and although he didn't know the correct ring size, he believed it might fit or he could have it resized if necessary.

"Well, I hope you have more than one of those rings, because I'll take that one, and I hope there is still another around for you someday."

While driving to Abilene, Stan thought about how he would present the ring to Melanie and decided not to give it to her during dinner with her parents. *This should be a private moment,* he thought and decided to find a way to give it to her before taking them all to dinner.

He had grown accustomed to the trip and loved the hardly travelled roads as he journeyed past open land with clear sky above. It made him think of the hours spent flying over this terrain and the thrill of maneuvering in practice areas above him. The sight of an occasional T-37 or T-38 made him feel proud that he was part of something so much bigger than just himself. He was part of an organization he considered above the ordinary. Imagine having to wake up every morning, walk to a bus stop, board a crowded bus to New York City, take a subway, and then walk to an office building to spend eight or nine hours before making a return trip. That is exactly what his father had been doing for decades and was still doing. *My God,* he thought, I'm so lucky. *Thank God I have not been sentenced to such a mundane existence.* Then he thought, *Thanks Dad, you did that for us.*

Time alone during these trips was both cathartic and enjoyable. It gave him plenty of time to reflect upon what he had done recently and what he intended to do. He wanted to fine tune his cockpit procedure and improve his overall performance as a pilot. Cockpit instrumentation, radio procedure, approach chart information, frequencies of navigational aids, and a myriad of other concerns occupying the aviation section of his mind were frequently interspersed with thoughts of his life with Melanie. Both had become so important to him and he thought of them both as his duty, and nothing was more important to him than the performance of his duty.

As he drove along the now familiar unpaved roadway toward the Blakes' home, he realized that the trip to the restaurant might be rather uncomfortable for four people in his Firebird since there was not much room on the rear seat. It was fine for agile, well-conditioned, young people like himself, but for Melanie's parents, it might be a problem. Should they take her parents' car?

Melanie saw his car approaching the front of the house and waited for him on the porch. She ran to him as he exited the vehicle and they embraced.

"Where are Mom and Dad?" he asked. "Do we have a minute alone?"

"They're inside. Sure, we have a minute."

The gallant young man then made the obligatory one knee drop, took the ring from his pocket, gently lifted Melanie's hand, and placed the ring at the tip of her ring finger saying, "Miss Blake, will you marry me?"

"I already said I would! Now put the ring on already."

He could see that his charming young lady genuinely loved her engagement ring. She said it was perfect and that she could not have chosen a better one herself.

Stan was relieved that she was so happy. He kissed her and said, "One thing to clear up, Miss Blake. How are you going to feel about being called Mrs. Marks?"

"That's a real hoot. Are you kidding? I've been rehearsing it for months now and I already think of myself as Mrs. Marks. Melanie Marks…nice ring to it…don't you think? I love it."

"Are your mom and dad ready for dinner?"

"Boy, Mom and I have been in the kitchen for hours preparing a small feast."

"What? But I thought we were going out to a restaurant?"

"So did I, but Mom would not hear of it. She wanted to do something special for us and Dad went out and bought a nice bottle of champagne."

"You mean…they…?"

"Yup, they know. Sorry, but I was so excited that I just couldn't keep my mouth shut. They are so happy for us."

"Yes, but I didn't even…"

"Tell me? C'mon Stan, I can read you like a book. I just knew you were bringing me a ring today and I've been dying to see it ever since I received your last letter."

They walked into the house together and Mrs. Blake looked at Melanie. Her daughter's eyes sparkled and her face radiated with joy. She then ran to Stan, threw her arms around him, and gave him a big hug. After seeing the ring on Melanie's finger, she remarked on its beauty and complimented her fiancé on his excellent choice.

Mr. Blake walked up to his friend, shook his hand, and said, "Welcome home, son."

When he had the opportunity, he whispered to Melanie, "Thank God I brought the ring with me."

After enjoying a celebratory meal with champagne, the ladies entered the kitchen and Mr. Blake invited his soon to be son-in-law into the living room for a cigar and brandy. The old soldier regaled him as usual with stories of World War II adventures in the Philippine Islands. He repeated himself on occasion, but Stan thoroughly enjoyed listening to tales of camaraderie and what Mr. Blake made sound like a great adventure.

Wanting to know more about what really happened in those jungles, he attempted to extract details and started asking questions regarding contact with the enemy and about survival techniques in jungle warfare. But, he sensed a change in the old warrior's mood and decided to restrict the subject to his enjoyment of the cigar and brandy. The last thing he wanted to do was put any kind of damper on such a wonderful occasion.

Jeff Blake knew why he wanted more information and promised him that they would discuss the matter at some future time. "I'll look forward to that, sir," said Stan.

Melanie emerged from the kitchen and commandeered her fiancé from her father. The new couple spent time together in their usual place on the front porch and discussed their future. They talked about flight school graduation scheduled in a few months, and decided that would be a good time for the wedding.

Many questions occupied their minds since Stan would not be informed regarding future assignments until just prior to graduation. However, they did not have to consider living arrangements since, as an Air Force officer on active duty, Melanie would be residing at Cannon Air Force Base in New Mexico. She would continue her current living arrangements on base with visits to her family in Abilene.

As for the wedding, Melanie preferred a simple civil ceremony and a small reception at her family home. If they could arrange leave simultaneously, they could take a short honeymoon, at a location to be determined after the wedding. Happy with their plans, they enjoyed the remainder of their weekend and returned to their respective bases.

7

Stan was now flying solo and flight planning his own missions with the approval of instructors prior to entering training areas. He was now instrument rated also, meaning that he was qualified to fly under instrument flight rules (IFR) during poor weather conditions as opposed to visual flight rules (VFR) during good conditions. He had also experienced flying at night. Landing his aircraft at night during IFR conditions was a thrilling experience requiring discipline and coordination.

Ground controlled approaches (GCAs) using ground based precision approach radar (PAR) and the guidance of radio transmissions provided by air traffic controllers gave him glide path and azimuth information until he broke out of the cloud layers and was able to see runway approach lights and take over visually for landing. Ground based instrument landing systems (ILS) approaches provided similar information without the aid of ground based controllers, however, there was nothing better than that professional controller with a calm voice telling him that he was on glide path and on course. If his aircraft ever ventured above or below glide path or to the left or right of course, the controller immediately advised him to correct. When his aircraft reached minimum descent altitude for the approach and he still did not have the runway environment in sight, the controller told him to execute a missed approach and they tried it over again.

About one month prior to graduation, Stan was returning to base during daytime VFR conditions. After the approach controller instructed him to contact the control tower prior to final approach for landing, he lowered his landing gear. Indications on his cockpit instrument panel indicated that his nose gear and left main gear were down. However, his right main gear did not appear to be down. He retracted his landing gear and tried again. Once again, he received a bad indication on his right main gear and notified the tower of his situation. He asked the tower controllers to check his gear visually as he executed a low approach, flew past the tower and down the length of the runway, without touching down on the pavement. The controller notified him that his right main gear did not appear to be down. He gained a little altitude off the departure end of the runway and began to rock his wings and maneuver his nose up and down multiple times in an attempt to shake the errant gear loose, to no avail.

After exhausting all possible means of lowering his gear, Stan contacted Lariat, the RSU for T-38 training, and notified them regarding his situation. The instructor pilot on duty had observed the problem as the aircraft flew by and told him to fly an approach to the runway under his control and to touch down on the runway using only his two available landing gear in an attempt to dislodge his right main gear and then execute a touch and go. This meant that he should touch down on his left main gear and then apply power to again become airborne. He completed another flight pattern and executed the maneuver as instructed. The gear did not jar loose and he was told to recycle his gear once again. And again, this did not work.

His aircraft was still in the pattern and ground personnel were able to view his operation. The RSU inquired regarding fuel remaining on board his aircraft and time available for flight. The supervisor decided that he should try to touch down on the runway a little harder and go around again. This was getting a little tense by now and the base emergency equipment had been alerted. The equipment and personnel were being positioned near the runway being used by Stan in the event they were needed.

He had apparently responded well to his training. It was obvious to ground personnel that he was in control of his aircraft and following prescribed procedure. Lieutenant Marks knew that he could not attempt to land his aircraft utilizing only a nose gear and one main gear because his plane would cartwheel. He would not only destroy the aircraft, but would jeopardize ground personnel and equipment. He himself would go the same route as his plane.

The T-38 touched down on the runway again and this time harder. He then applied power and climbed toward the departure end of the runway. His cockpit gear indications did not change and the RSU notified him that his gear was still not extended. He was again instructed to recycle his gear, and again the situation did not change.

Fuel remaining aboard his aircraft was now a definite issue. These jet aircraft burn fuel much more quickly at low altitude and that is where he had been for a while. Lieutenant Marks was directed to remain in the pattern and await further instructions. A very short time later, a familiar voice used his aircraft call sign. He recognized the voice as that of an instructor pilot who gave a block of instruction on cockpit ejection procedure.

The airspace around the base and surrounding area was cleared of all unnecessary air traffic and all operational personnel were put on alert status. The instructor informed the lieutenant that he was going to have to eject from his aircraft since that was the best option available. They went through a thorough checklist and he was directed to a desolate area a few miles from the base and told to climb to an altitude of 8,500 feet.

While proceeding to the area designated for ejection, he was briefed regarding proper trim settings to have the aircraft maintain level flight and his position inside the aircraft prior to ejection. Lieutenant Marks was a well-built but tall young man and there was very little space available in the cockpit of his aircraft. He was surrounded by metal equipment and the severe force generated by the blast beneath his seat during ejection demanded that all parts of his body remain clear of the cramped cockpit interior to ensure that no body parts were left behind.

Stan was relaying his navigational aid (NAVAID) equipment and distance measuring equipment (DME) information to the supervisors as he approached the point of ejection. Rescue personnel had already been dispatched to that location. A supervisor gave him final instructions for equipment adjustments and for landing on the ground after parachute deployment. After a thorough checklist was reviewed, he was given the green light to eject.

The pilot's only thought at this time was of surviving this ordeal and being with Melanie again. He was determined to do this right. He pulled his body in as far as he could from the interior of the aircraft and armed the aircraft ejection system by pulling up on handles located at both sides of his seat and squeezing the trigger mechanism. The aircraft canopy jettisoned and a ferocious blast ensued as his seat rose along rails fitted inside the cockpit for the proper initial trajectory.

Lieutenant Marks was stunned by the sound of the blast, the G-forces exerted upon his body, and the tension exerted by the harnesses holding him in place. His seat fell away from his body; he felt a very hard jerk as his parachute canopy deployed and he watched the final moments of his aircraft descent prior to its impact in an open and unoccupied area. *This is why military installations are usually located in sparsely populated areas,* he thought. The loss of such a valuable asset made him shudder and he could not help but feel pangs of guilt. He could not help but wonder if there was anything more he could have done to prevent such a loss.

As he approached the ground, he did not feel a thing and his mind was racing. *Geez, I'm still alive,* he thought. But he then realized that he had never hit the dirt from a parachute fall before. He now became concerned with the terrain below him, and he did not see a problem. Stan remembered that he was supposed to make ground contact with the side of a foot, rather than touchdown flat-footed or on the heel of his feet to prevent injury, to tuck his knees, and to roll over onto his side, and then his shoulder area.

"Damn, I did it," he said after getting on his feet and wrestling to get free of his parachute harness. As he looked around, he was amazed to see personnel and equipment racing to his location. *Wow, is this outfit great or what?* he thought.

The jettisoned pilot was escorted into a van where he was attended to by emergency personnel. He appeared to be free of serious injury, but en route to the base medical facilities he began feeling somewhat nauseous and aches were developing at various parts of his body. Extreme emotional and physical stress began taking its toll as the adrenaline rush subsided. At the base, he was given a thorough physical exam and his only ailments were in the form of bruises, abrasions, and pulled muscles. He was a lucky man indeed, and he knew it.

Stan had just experienced what no fighter pilot wants, and he lived to tell about it. This made him suddenly a much more valuable member of his organization and debriefings following the event were extensive in attempts to extract information useful for training of future personnel and for possible improvements to equipment and procedure.

8

News of such events spread very quickly throughout military organizations. Personnel are transferred frequently to meet mission requirements and, as a result, networks are established throughout the country and globally. That very day, Melanie was working in her office at her base in New Mexico when she was notified by a co-worker that the squadron commander wished to see her. When she appeared at the open door of the major's office, he stood up and asked her to have a seat. He then closed the door and said, "Lieutenant Blake, I understand that you were recently engaged to be married. Is that right?"

"Yes sir, it is."

"I just learned this and would like to offer you my congratulations."

"Thank you, sir."

"I understand that the young man is in pilot training at Laughlin, is that correct?"

"Yes sir."

"May I ask his name?"

"It's Lieutenant Stanley Marks, sir."

"Your young man is very lucky in more ways than one."

"Sir?"

"Don't be alarmed. He's alright, but he was forced to eject from his aircraft."

"What? Oh no. Are you sure he's okay?"

"Quite sure. I just want you to know that you need not worry and that I will make leave available for you if and when you need it. Just ask."

Melanie needed a moment to collect her thoughts and bring her emotional state under control. Her eyes began to well with tears and she then said, with as controlled a voice as she was able to muster, "Sir, Stan and I plan to marry next month after he earns his wings, and we would both like to arrange for some leave at that time."

"I'm sure that can be arranged, Lieutenant, and please convey my congratulations to Lieutenant Marks as well."

During the incident, Stan's roommates, Eric and Rich, had been aware of events in real time. Eric had been monitoring the occurrence from his squadron operations building and Rich was on duty at the RAPCON directing his crew during the emergency. Rich had been flight-following the aircraft on radar and when the target disappeared, he had the controller mark the spot on his scope with a black grease pencil to permit his controllers to vector rescue aircraft to that location in case it became necessary.

Neither Eric nor Rich knew of the final outcome for a while and both were extremely anxious until they heard the good news. Now that their buddy was back in their midst, they planned a celebration. Not only was pilot training about to be successfully completed, but Stan was about to be married after surviving ejection from a supersonic jet aircraft. They were one hell of an ecstatic group.

The three musketeers spent a wonderful day together water skiing on the lake. It was a day they would never forget as long as they lived. The sun shone as bright as their hopes were for the future. Their boating and water skiing exploits that day were as daring and as exciting as they imagined their futures. They attempted and, in some cases, were successful at water skiing maneuvers that had previously been beyond their ability. At the end of a fun-filled day, before the sun receded, they stowed their gear, turned off the engine, and allowed the boat to float in the middle of the lake. Rich then opened a cooler packed with a bottle of champagne on ice and three glasses. They toasted each other on their past accomplishments and future goals. A bond had been established sealing them together no matter where they went and no matter what they were called upon to endure.

Lieutenant Marks was amazed at the correspondence he was receiving as a result of his ejection. Some of it was in the form of official requests for additional information, but most of it was from family members, friends, former classmates, instructors, and acquaintances. His brother Pat told him that he had become something of a celebrity at his old college and that cadets and instructors all took pride in his success. Stan thought that his 'success' may have been more a matter of being lucky than being good but hoped that, if that were the case, luck would always be his companion.

The letter he received from Army Captain Bart Small was an eye opener. His unit was currently undergoing advanced training prior to deployment to Vietnam. Bart congratulated his friend and told him that he had consumed several scotch and waters in celebration of his successful cockpit ejection. That made him smile, but he then thought about what lay ahead for his pal Bart. It seemed as though America was spending an inordinate amount of time and resources preparing its youth for deployment to a small country that most had never even heard of. Hell, even fewer knew where the place was.

However, he held firm in his conviction that this was something that needed to be done.

Just prior to the long-awaited wing pinning day, when the newly rated Air Force pilots receive the wings proudly worn on their uniforms, the student pilots were given their aircraft assignments. Stan and Eric were assigned to O-2 Skymaster training at Hurlburt Field in Florida. They were going to train for forward air control duties. Prior to that training, they would attend survival school at Fairchild Air Force Base in Washington State for approximately three weeks. He scheduled one week of leave following graduation from pilot training prior to reporting to Fairchild. Stan wrote a letter to Melanie asking that she make arrangements for her leave and the wedding.

Melanie had been flying high for quite some time now and felt as though she had earned her wings as well. She was about to marry the man she admired and loved. He took care to make her happy and was working hard to prepare for a good future. Better than that, he was dedicated to things more important than just himself and that was especially meaningful to her since it was something she herself strived toward.

Stan's parents, Melanie, Mr. and Mrs. Blake, Fred, and Ann, were all present at the graduation and they witnessed the wing pinning. Stan had not seen his parents for quite some time and knew it would not be easy for them to make their way from New Jersey to Texas for the ceremony and the wedding. He did not expect them to come, but they did drive all the way and it took them five days to make the trip. And of course, there was still the return trip to consider. They decided to make it a vacation since neither of them had ever taken such a trip before in their entire lives. His brothers and sister would have liked to attend, but school was in session and the costs were prohibitive.

His mom and dad took many pictures to bring home for relatives and friends and they seemed so pleased to finally meet the Melanie they had read about in letters and the wonderful parents their son raved about. They, like Stan, fell in love with Melanie and told her parents about the wonderful things their son said about them in his letters home. From Del Rio, the group travelled to Abilene for the wedding ceremony and reception scheduled to take place at the Blake Ranch the following day.

The ceremony took place outdoors in front of the Blake family home and was as simple as Melanie had wanted. However, the occasion was somewhat spectacular in that the bride was so beautiful in her traditional, white wedding gown and veil. Lieutenant Marks was in full dress uniform, which was very much a military-style tuxedo, and he proudly wore his newly acquired wings. His roommates and many other military officers, also in full dress uniform, were present. Fred, accompanied by Ann, was in uniform as well.

Stan's mom remarked that she felt as though she was watching a movie. She had never experienced anything like this before and found it very impressive. His dad was all smiles and practically speechless. Melanie pointed out to Stan that their fathers appeared to be getting along well. "Just look at them. Two peas in a pod. They are both such good, decent, human beings. We are so lucky." Although a very strict disciplinarian, Stan always knew that his dad was and would always be there for them. "And look at our moms," remarked Melanie. "Seems we didn't do too badly in that department either."

During the reception, Mr. Blake called his son-in-law aside and as they strolled through the property, he shared a story with him. He explained that the property had been in his family for generations and that it had once encompassed a much larger area. It had been a cattle ranch belonging to his great grandfather and over the years, the land had been passed down to descendants. Most of the land had been sold off by preceding generations; however, the remaining five hundred acres belonged to him and Mrs. Blake. He showed Stan a section of land, including a pond, rolling hills, and some trees.

"See that area over there?" he asked. "Melanie learned to ride horses over there and she has loved riding there ever since."

"Yes, I know, she taught me to ride there as well. Seems to me that we always went to the same place."

"I can imagine. That was always her favorite space. She seems at peace there and we love seeing how happy she is when she rides there. Well, that area is about a hundred acres and it now belongs to you and Melanie."

"What? What do you mean?"

"I mean it's a wedding present. We've already had the legal papers drawn up. Maybe you two will build something for yourselves over there someday."

"Wow. I really love it here. This is a great place to raise a family. Is this for real? Does Melanie know about this?"

"You bet it's for real and nothing would make us happier than to see you raise a family there. Now let's go talk to your wife."

After all the guests had departed that evening, Mr. and Mrs. Blake announced that they had planned a vacation and were leaving that night. Their bags were already packed and in the car. With a twinkle in their eyes, they said their goodbyes, embraced the newlyweds, and left the young couple alone at the family home.

Stan and Melanie honeymooned at the homestead; they took long walks, rode horses, and enjoyed this time alone together as they planned their future. Their dream was to build a home on their newly acquired property. They discussed what type of house it would be and where on the property it should be built. At this early stage, they even considered drainage, shade, sunrise, and riding trails. Their minds were filled with hope and anticipation. Both of them wanted children and imagined teaching them to ride on the same trails where they themselves learned. They even considered the possibility of constructing a short dirt runway that could be used for a small single engine aircraft.

The week went by fast, much too fast, and it was soon time for them to leave. Lieutenant Marks packed only essentials into his car for the trip to Washington State. Melanie knew that he would return in three weeks, and that they would have a little more time together before he had to depart again to Florida for additional training.

Since Melanie was an Air Force personnel officer, she was well aware of the hardships associated with being a military spouse, but she was also human and she was a newlywed. She did not like being separated from her husband, especially since they were just married. How could she remedy this situation? What were her options?

9

The trip to Fairchild Air Force Base in Washington State took Lieutenant Marks across yet another part of the country that he had never before seen. He only wished that he were able to share this adventure with Melanie. She was back at her base in New Mexico and it would be about two and a half more years before her Air Force commitment was fulfilled and the newlyweds could plan a future together.

It was a beautiful trip and one he would have gladly planned as a vacation. The changes in scenery were at times breathtaking and he was once again fulfilling childhood dreams. He felt some guilt at his joy whenever he thought about being away from his bride, and that was often.

Eric joined Stan at the base and they were both happy to have another buddy along for the ride, although there were a few familiar faces from their pilot training class. This survival school class was mainly comprised of new pilots sent from a number of pilot training bases throughout the country.

The training, called survival, evasion, resistance, and escape training (SERE) was even more comprehensive and exhausting than he anticipated. Sleep deprivation, hunger, exposure to the elements for days and nights at a time, and how to survive such conditions were to be expected as part of the training. He was also taught about emergency medical self-treatment in the event of injury after ejection, and given additional instruction in parachute techniques after ejection. *Better late than never,* he thought. They were also exposed to methods of evading capture, building shelters in the woods, procuring edible food, how to behave if captured, and possible methods of escape.

During this training, he recalled his attempt to extract information from Mr. Blake regarding his experiences in the jungles of the Philippine Islands during World War II. He had since learned that if he were deployed to the war zone, he would first be sent to a jungle survival training course at Clark Air Force Base in the Philippines en route to Vietnam. But he would never ask Mr. Blake about those experiences again for fear of having him recall painful events. That Army veteran would have to volunteer information of his own accord.

Completion of this course left its attendees hoping they would never, ever have to put what they had just learned into practice. *But,* the lieutenant thought, *almost everything I have ever learned thus far has been of help to me at one time or another or in one form or another. I sure am glad this is over and I can't wait to see Melanie again.* He had written to let her know when to expect him in Abilene and headed in that direction at the first possible opportunity.

While driving toward the house, he could see Melanie standing on the front porch waiting for him. The view from the front of the home to the main roadway at the end of the long unpaved road allowed someone to view an approaching vehicle from quite a distance and his bright red sports car really stood out. There was no question. It could not have been anyone else but him. Melanie was waving and smiling as he got closer. He stopped his car, jumped out, left his driver's-side door open, and they ran to each other delivering warm embraces and kisses as they attempted to make up for all the lost moments of the past few weeks.

The time they had together was very short and very passionate. The ejection incident, although hardly ever mentioned, made them realize the extent to which they needed to savor such precious moments.

That evening, the young couple had a discussion regarding the all-too-frequent separations required of them. Initiating the conversation, Stan said, "Melanie, we need to work something out. Personnel officers are stationed at almost every air base. When I finally get a stateside permanent change of station, we need to see if we can get posted together. Right now, all I'm getting are temporary assignments. That will change someday and we should try to coordinate that move so we can be based together."

"You must be a mind reader, Stan. I've been thinking about that a lot lately. As soon as you get word of a permanent assignment where I can come with you, I will try to work it out."

"Don't worry, we'll figure it out together," he stated. "Right now, I need to concentrate on my assignment to Hurlburt Field in Florida for O-2 qualification training."

"And we know that upon completion of that assignment, you will be going to Vietnam for a year. We have to face it," she answered.

"That is what I'm being trained for, Melanie. We need to really make the best of this time together and have faith that things will eventually change for the better. We both chose this life. We'll be okay. Count on it."

Mrs. Marks knew what she was getting into when she married an Air Force pilot. None of this came as a surprise to her, but that did not help ease the pain. She was hurting and she was terrified. However, when the time came for him to leave, she put on a brave face and gave him a prolonged embrace, concealing her heartache.

Fortunately, her mother was there to comfort her. She was well aware of her daughter's suffering since she herself lived through a similar experience.

"Melanie, I was carrying you when your father was away in the war."

"I know, Mom. How did you get through it?"

"Well, I won't lie to you, it wasn't easy. But I'll tell you this – if I could get through it, you can too and you'll be a better and a stronger person for it."

10

The distance from Abilene, Texas, to Hurlburt Field, Florida, was about 850 miles and Stan was making another trip alone. He was not happy about leaving his wife behind again, but Lieutenant Melanie Marks was also performing her military duty in accordance with the needs of the service.

Stan was now somewhat familiar with the countryside he traversed during this journey. However, Florida presented another new adventure and his wife would have loved to make the trip. Before his marriage, the Air Force had been the most important thing in his life, but he now had something just as important to consider and it occupied his mind continually on this journey.

Hurlburt Field is located in the Florida Panhandle along the Gulf Coast in close proximity to Eglin Air Force Base. He had been told the beaches in the area were beautiful and the area was a tourist attraction. Nice information, but he would have preferred sharing all of this with his new bride. An interesting assignment indeed, but the enemy he now faced was loneliness.

The O-2 is the military version of the Cessna 337 Skymaster known by Air Force personnel as the Duck or the Oscar Deuce. It has twin tail booms giving it a unique appearance. The aircraft has what is called a push-pull engine configuration meaning that one piston-powered engine is located at the nose of the aircraft and another such engine at its rear, giving it a centerline thrust for more efficient control as opposed to two engines, one located on each wing. The aircraft has high wings allowing pilots clear observation below and behind it

The O-2 was an improvement over the O-1 in that it has two engines. In the event one engine failed, it was still able to fly with the other operating, although not as well. It flew better when the rear engine was operating rather than the other way around. When the O-1 lost an engine, it was, "Oh well, where do I put this sucker down." In Vietnam, that was usually not a good thing.

The aircraft was also equipped with ordinance hard points under its wings for rocket and machine gun pods. An armament control panel, including a gun sight, was also provided. The O-2 usually carried seven folding fin rockets in each of two pods equipped with white phosphorous (WP) 'Willie Pete' heads. The rockets were utilized by forward air controllers to mark locations to be attacked by fighter aircraft called to the scene and they emitted large plumes of white smoke to identify the areas where fighter pilots needed to respond.

FACs piloting these aircraft were trained to operate three different sets of radio equipment to perform their duties satisfactorily. FM radios were provided for contact with troop commanders on the ground needing support, VHF radios for contact with a tactical air control party (TACP) locating and sending fighter aircraft, and UHF radios for contact with the fighter pilots sent to the scene. Successful coordination of this radio equipment while keeping track of the action on the ground and simultaneously avoiding enemy ground fire is what a good FAC does.

Lieutenant Marks loved the flight characteristics of his new flying machine. It performed as he imagined it would and he loved flying low and slow. It allowed him to take in the local landmarks and to enjoy the scenery. The scenery at his new base was breathtaking. The beaches along the Gulf Coast were beautiful indeed, but he felt guilty spending time there when he did manage to get to the beach. His mind was always on what he now considered to be 'back home' and that meant with the new Mrs. Marks.

Eric was also training along with Stan at Hurlburt and they resumed their old informal training techniques applied at flight school. They kept exchanging roles as ground commanders, FACs, fighter pilots, and TACP personnel. The roleplay occasionally got out of hand as they laughed and started to become 'salty' with phraseology. One of them would always pipe up and imitate Rich, their air traffic control buddy, declaring, "Clean up that phraseology, you bums, or you are both confined to barracks this weekend." That usually called for a beer along with a toast to their good buddy Rich.

Both men were becoming very good pilots and were starting to gain proficiency with the equipment aboard their aircraft. Firing their rockets at practice ranges was another surreal adventure providing an almost amusement park like environment for overgrown children not yet exposed to the real hazards involved in what they were being trained to accomplish.

The instructors were mostly veterans of the current Southeast Asia conflict and gave valuable insight to the as yet uninitiated. They squashed some of the silliness exhibited by 'newbies' with serious facial expressions and by forcefully imparting information obtained during combat experience. Any evidence of overconfidence or arrogance was met with disapproval.

Among the many valuable tidbits imparted to students not yet exposed to a combat environment included information such as placing a mark on their aircraft windshield with a black grease pencil rather than using their gun sights for weapon firing accuracy. That reduced cockpit distraction and provided about the same degree of accuracy. All of these seemingly small lessons, with repetition over a period of time, made the pilots much more proficient as they gradually became as one with their machines.

Correspondence with family and friends, especially with Melanie, along with the friendship and camaraderie of his new classmates, made life more pleasant and provided a much-needed antidote for loneliness and homesickness. He learned from Melanie that she had been recently promoted to first lieutenant, and he shared the same news with her regarding the promotions of Eric and himself to the same rank.

They were approaching completion of their certification training in their new 'office space' and were about to become proud masters of their flying 'Ducks.' Each pilot developed personal techniques concerning coordination of radio equipment transmission, armament procedure inside the cockpit, and the building of their personal 'nests.' They placed items such as flight charts, writing instruments, canteens, weapons, and other items, depending upon the personal preferences of the individual involved, in ergonomically correct positions to meet their personal needs.

The newly qualified O-2 pilots learned that every situation encountered in the combat environment could differ and that the extent of their ingenuity, resourcefulness, and perseverance would be called upon repeatedly in the performance of their duty. Procedure was important and must be followed during routine events, but what they were training for was anything but routine. They could not expect to learn a procedure to be followed for every situation encountered. Each pilot needed to determine a course of action affecting not only himself, but others both in the air as well as on the ground.

When the training was nearing its end, the pilots received their orders and assignments. As expected, they were all going to various locations in Vietnam. There was a shortage of FACs and they were urgently needed in the war zone. None of the pilots expected anything other than the inevitable outcome; the only question was where were they going in Vietnam?

Both Stan and Eric were assigned to the Tactical Air Support Squadron (TASS) at Da Nang Air Base. That base was in I Corps, the northernmost of the three largest air bases in South Vietnam. The other two large bases were Cam Ranh Bay and Tan Son Nhut located further south. En route to the war zone, both were scheduled to attend Jungle Survival School at Clark Air Base in the Philippines.

He wrote to Melanie and let her know when to expect him back home in Abilene, but he did not inform her about his new assignment.

Prior to receiving his orders, he learned that Bart Small's unit had been deployed to Vietnam. Captain Small would also be operating in the I Corps region and this led Stan to believe he may be of some future assistance to his old cadet commander after all. However, he may never know it because his friend's unit could be almost anywhere in that region.

Lieutenant Marks was becoming more and more aware that it was imperative for him to remain alert in order to assist soldiers on the ground in need of air support. As a matter of fact, that was something Bart stressed during their last encounter at Fort Bragg. "Always be there for the people you are responsible for," he said, or words to that effect.

It was finally time to head back to his Texas home and the newly qualified O-2 jockey bid a temporary farewell to his ole buddy Eric. "See you in Snake School" was the parting expression they used to describe the jungle survival training they were slated to attend.

11

Back in the proverbial saddle, Stan was tearing up the roadway westward on his way back home to the lovely Mrs. Marks and Texas. This time it was not with the heavy heart he experienced while driving east toward Hurlburt. He had not been in as much of a hurry during the trip to Florida as he was while driving toward Abilene. The sooner he arrived, the more time he had to spend with Melanie before heading off to jungle survival school en route to Vietnam. He had one week before reporting to Norton Air Force Base in California and board a flight to the Philippines.

While driving home, he thought about R&R (Rest and Recuperation). One week was provided by the military for soldiers during Vietnam tours. The soldiers with the most time in country were selected first for R&R and it usually took at least six months of service before it would be approved. After eight months, approval was pretty much assured. There were a number of destinations soldiers could pick from for their R&R. The single guys usually went to Australia, Thailand, or Taiwan, and the married guys typically went to Hawaii where they would meet with their wives.

They didn't really have very much of a honeymoon and in an attempt to brighten Melanie's spirits, he decided to plan a Hawaii honeymoon with her. She loved to plan for the future and he recalled her smile and how her eyes lit up when they discussed plans to build a home on the Texas property. He wanted to see her that happy again and thought this might do the trick.

During his westbound journey, a radio broadcast disturbed his train of thought and he wanted to know more about what was happening. He turned up the volume and heard something about a shooting at Kent State University. As he listened more closely, he learned that students protesting the war and, more specifically U.S. bombing in Cambodia, had been shot by National Guardsmen. American university students had been shot and some had been killed by members of a United States military organization. *How can this be?* he thought. *The U.S. military protects American citizens. How can this be happening?* It was not that long ago that he and Melanie were both college students and were now members of the U.S. military. As American soldiers, was it not their sworn duty to protect the rights of these students to protest? *Something is terribly wrong here. This is not right.*

His mind was like a volcano about to erupt. He changed the radio station to one of soothing music and took a deep breath. *These emotions are not doing me or anyone else any good,* he realized as he slowly reduced his temperature and began to simmer down. His thoughts returned to the immediate task at hand, getting back home to Melanie.

Stan didn't want to lose any time and drove continually, only stopping for fuel. Sandwiches, drinks, and snacks were packed in a cooler on the seat next to him, so there was no need to stop for food.

Departing the Florida Panhandle at 0300 hours, he planned to arrive in Abilene at about 1600 hours. He did a little better and reached the unpaved road toward the front door at about

1530 hours. That's 3:30 p.m., still giving him some time with Melanie before the end of that day.

One of the benefits of long separation is the joy and celebration of reunion. Happier people one would never expect to see. Melanie's face was glowing and she looked more beautiful than ever. The atmosphere was exceptionally joyous as the ladies prepared a huge feast for the returning warrior.

Stan appreciated a good home-cooked meal, and dinner was delicious as usual. Satisfied and content, he sat back and delighted his new family with tales of his aviation adventures and the good friends he made along the way.

Everyone listened intently, but he had a feeling that something was different. He couldn't quite put his finger on it, but it seemed to him that they were all preoccupied. His father-in-law was friendly and fairly quiet as usual, but he could see by the little smile on his face and the twinkle in his eyes that something was on his mind.

Following that superb dinner, Stan and Melanie strolled out to the front porch to be alone. They had so much to talk about.

"When are you leaving, Stan?"

"I have five days before I leave for California to catch a flight to the Philippines for survival school."

"And then to Vietnam?"

"Yes, I'll be with Eric at Da Nang. Seems like they always cut our orders together. It's nice to know there will be a familiar face when I get there. I wonder if you know how much I've missed you since I was last here; it was really hard."

"I know. It wasn't easy for me either. Listen, Stan, I have something very important to tell you."

"Okay, what is it?"

"I'm not going to be in the Air Force much longer."

"Really? What happened?"

Melanie was suddenly beaming and could no longer keep her secret. She smiled at him lovingly, squeezed his hand, and exclaimed, "Stan…you are going to be a father."

"I am going to be a father," he repeated, as his eyes opened wide.

And again he repeated, "I am going to be a father," trying to let that sink in.

When it finally did sink in, he jumped up and said in a loud voice that was surely heard inside the house, "Oh that's what you said. You said that I'm going to be a father. Is that what you said?"

Melanie loved his reaction. She stood up and repeated, "Yes Stan. I said you are going to be a father."

He considered her delicate condition before throwing his arms around his wife and the child he could not wait to meet. Stan was going to be a father and he couldn't be happier!

Melanie admitted that she almost blurted out the news during dinner, but she wanted to be alone with him when she made the announcement.

Now that it was just the two of them, there was so much to discuss. She wanted him to know her plans and needed his approval. Several friends at Cannon Air Force Base suspected her pregnancy, so she intended to notify her squadron commander and begin out-processing from the Air Force immediately upon return to duty.

Melanie was so happy and excited to become a mother that she buried the reality of Vietnam deep in the back of her mind. She would think about that another day, because today was to celebrate. She informed Stan that her mom and dad were delighted about becoming grandparents and that she intended to live in the Abilene home after leaving the service; there was plenty of room in the house, and she would be well taken care of.

He had no doubt that she would be fine and he more than approved of her plans. Stan was stunned, thrilled, and relieved. His wife would be in a loving, secure environment during his combat tour. That was one less worry and it gave him some much-needed peace of mind.

Before leaving for his Vietnam tour, however, there was some business to take care of. The Firebird would remain at the Blake Ranch, and he wanted to change his vehicle registration and his driver's license from New Jersey to Texas before departing the country. Also, considering that he would need very little money during the next year, he wanted to open a joint account with Melanie and set up an allotment to deposit the majority of his income for her use during his absence.

As he explained these plans to his wife, she was filled with gratitude for the love of this remarkable man. With his mind still racing, he asked, "The baby will arrive in about six months, right?"

"About that time, yes."

"Perfect," he said, "After the baby is born and you are feeling up to it, I'll apply for R&R and we are going to have a real honeymoon in Hawaii."

Melanie was ecstatic. She knew that her parents would be willing and happy to take care of the baby. The thought of R&R with her husband in Hawaii after the baby was born eased some of the pain of separation. They could enjoy a whole week together in one of the most beautiful places on Earth.

Time seemed to fly by since there was so much to do before he had to leave. Stan did find a little time to spend with his father-in-law, but the gentleman did not speak much about his wartime experiences in the Philippines. All he would say was that Stan needed to learn as much as he could in survival school and to pay close attention to his instructors. He did mention that he believed it advisable for Stan to stay with his aircraft if at all possible because did not want to be on the ground in that environment.

Mr. Blake then said something very meaningful: "Remember, son, that is their home turf, it is not yours. You will be an intruder there. They know the lay of the land, you do not. It is their home, it is not yours, and they do not want you there. If they were here you would do all you could to kick them out. Do not expect any better treatment from them. They are going to be very serious. Do not leave that airplane if at all possible."

Stan thanked him for that advice and took it to heart.

Saying goodbye this time was incredibly hard. Melanie was in tears, unable to put on that brave face. Consoling her was difficult because Stan felt much the same way. He was not just leaving a new wife behind, he was also leaving his unborn child. This ranch had become home and he took one long look around before announcing, "It's going to take a while, but I am going to get back here, because I most definitely need to get back here." He gave his wife one more long embrace, said his good-byes to her mother, and entered Mr. Blake's pickup truck.

The tearful goodbye with his wife was very hard to take. Holding hands through the window of the truck, Stan reminded her that they would meet in Hawaii and everything would be fine. She seemed to cheer up a little, and Mr. Blake was able to drive down the dirt road, with the young couple waving until the truck was out of sight.

Lieutenant Marks was wearing his uniform as required to fly military standby on commercial flights, and his wings let the flight crews know that he was one of them. He only had one small bag with him because almost everything he needed would be provided when he reached his destinations. As the pickup truck left the unpaved surface and entered the main roadway for the trip to Abilene Regional Airport, Mr. Blake reached into his glove compartment and pulled out a flask. Handing it to his son-in-law, he said, "Brandy, son, here take a swig." Stan smiled, took a good long pull on the 'medicine jug,' and handed it back.

"Thank you, sir. Think I needed that."

Then Mr. Blake sipped a bit of the brandy himself and said, "So did I," before replacing the flask in the glove compartment.

"You know, Stan, I'm a retired high school teacher."

"Yes sir, I know that. What did you teach?"

"History. After the war, I had all the excitement I ever needed and loved working with youngsters. Wanted to teach them how important it was to live peaceful lives. Sometimes I wonder just how much of an impact I've had."

"I'll bet you were a great teacher. You've certainly taught me a lot in the short time I've known you and I appreciate your patience with a northern city-type like me."

"You, a northern city-type? Nah, you might be from up there, but you aren't at all what most folks around here think of them. As a matter of fact, I hear nothing but good things about you from people around here, and they all respect you for your service to our country."

"Well, that sure is nice to hear because I just may be here for some time when I get back home."

"That's really great to hear, son. Tell me, how much do you know about the people and the country you are going to?"

"Sad to say, not that much, sir. All I really know is that I'm going there to help protect the South Vietnamese from the threat of communist takeover."

"You know, Stan, the Vietnamese are a people that have been kicked around for decades. Before the Second World War, they had been a French possession, along with Laos, and Cambodia since the 1800s. Vietnam became a very important part of the French economy because of its resources such as tea, rubber, and indigo which the French exported for sale and profit. That continued until around 1940. During the Second World War, Germany occupied France and Japan wanted bases in Vietnam for their Asian conquests. The newly formed Vichy government in France acquiesced and Japan occupied Vietnam until the end of the war. I'm not sure, but the Japanese may have utilized the base you are going to at that time. Following World War II, the French wanted their old colony back; it had been very valuable to them. Well, Vietnam had been occupied by the French and the Japanese for decades and the Vietnamese wanted their freedom from foreign domination. The French didn't see it that way and went to war in Vietnam for about eight years before they were defeated by the Vietnamese at Dien Bien Phu in northwest Vietnam. After the Second World War, Vietnam had been divided into two countries as a result of the Geneva Accords. The north became communist and the south democratic. All that happened before American involvement over there."

"Hmm, sounds like the current Vietnamese population have known nothing but war."

"That's about the size of it. The domino theory was a major consideration in American foreign policy in the 1960s. The belief was that if one nation in Asia fell to communist domination, others would follow. In 1964, two U.S. Navy

114

destroyers were allegedly fired upon by North Vietnam resulting in the Gulf of Tonkin Resolution and an initial large deployment of U.S. forces just north of Da Nang."

"So, the Vietnamese have had to put up with the French, the Japanese, the French again, and now Americans?"

"You've got it, Stan. Any question as to why they may want to be left the hell alone at this point?"

"Sounds like you are really against this war."

"I'm a veteran of foreign war and I hate any war, not just this one. And I certainly am not against you doing what you need to do. None of this is your fault any more than it's my fault. We're just caught up in it and so are the Vietnamese. Difference is you will get to come home and those poor bastards have nowhere else to go."

"Wow, never looked at it that way before."

"I'm sure you've studied about the American Revolution against British rule. Right?"

"Yes, of course."

"Well, at that time, the British represented the most powerful military force the world had ever seen, much as we do today. They were scattered all over God's creation just as we are today. We here in the former British colonies were occupied by the King of England's powerful military. The colonists were theoretically no match for such superior forces, but what was the final outcome of that conflict?"

"I see."

"My point, Stan, is that you need to be very careful over there. Those folks have nothing to lose that they aren't already used to losing as a matter of course. They have known misery and despair all of their lives and they are going to be very tough opponents. We want you back here in one piece."

"Got it, sir. Nothing is going to keep me away from Melanie and my unborn child, sir."

"God bless you, son."

12

The flight to Los Angeles was uneventful, as was the long bus ride from the Los Angeles Airport to Norton Air Force Base in San Bernardino. Traveling alone gave Lieutenant Marks plenty of time to reflect on recent events. Melanie's pregnancy, her departure from the Air Force, the Kent State affair, Mr. Blake's history lesson, and the impending jungle survival training all flowed through his mind like flood waters over a dam. He was in a barrel heading toward Niagara's Horseshoe Falls and was determined to survive what appeared to be a never-ending descent toward an undetermined outcome.

While waiting for his flight in a large holding area at Norton Air Force Base, surrounded by GIs from seemingly all branches of the service, someone tapped him on the shoulder and said, "Ready for Snake School, ole boy?"

"Hey Eric, good to see you. How was leave?"

Being from Florida, Eric had not been far from his parents' home after completing training at Hurlburt Field and had a little more leave time to enjoy with friends and relatives prior to meeting up with Stan in California. Apparently Eric enjoyed a raucous ole time with old buddies while surfing, water skiing, and chasing girls before heading off on his current adventures.

Getting back together with Eric was exactly what the doctor ordered. He needed very much to screw his head back on straight to prepare for what lay ahead and crazy ole Eric was just the guy he needed to help him adjust to a frame of mind necessary to tackle insanity.

They were both pretty well beat by the time they boarded an aircraft for a long flight, which would refuel in Hawaii before continuing across the Pacific to Clark Air Base. Before taking a little power nap, he told Eric the good news, he was going to be a father, and they both enjoyed a little banter over that happy prospect. Always on the lookout for a cause to celebrate, Eric announced that drinks were on him when they arrived at the airport terminal in Hawaii.

As the aircraft approached the Hawaiian Islands, the view of clear, blue water was nothing short of spectacular. Stan was in awe of this beautiful sight and remarked that the next time he flew to Hawaii, it would be to meet Melanie for R&R.

Eric smiled and responded light-heartedly, "That's great. Me…I'm planning R&R in Sydney, Australia. I'm dying to check out the chicks 'Down Under.' Or, are they 'birds' down there?"

"Yeah, well, let's not forget. Before all that we both have dates with a couple of hot 'Ducks.'"

There was only enough time at the airport terminal to enjoy one drink together before boarding their aircraft destined for the Philippines. While in the terminal area, Lieutenant Marks looked around at all the servicemen he had been with on the airplane wondering how many of them would survive to make a return trip. Of course, he would never know, especially since these guys represented all branches of the service and hardly any of them knew or trained with each other. Unlike previous wars, these soldiers were all replacements for other guys rotating out of their Vietnam assignments. Once Stan and Eric reached their final destination at Da Nang, it was unlikely that they would know anyone else in their squadron. But at least they had each other.

Approaching the Philippine Islands was a real eye opener for Stan. He was amazed at the number of those islands and imagined Mr. Blake and his Uncle Ben, another veteran of the war against Japan, fighting there. They had actually been down there in those jungles. He thought about how their experiences not only affected their lives but the lives of those they encountered following the war. These conflicts do not end when the war is over by any stretch of the imagination. Returning soldiers carry their experiences back home with them whether they realize it or not. He thought that Mr. Blake and his Uncle Ben handled their return to civilian life admirably but neither of them spoke much about it and tried to avoid such discussions. For better or worse, it appeared that they internalized their feelings and may have spent years suppressing and trying to forget as much as possible.

Looking at those islands, he could see how it was possible for surviving Japanese soldiers to avoid contact with the outside world for many years not knowing that the war had ended. *So many places to hide down there,* he thought, *how could you ever find them all?*

Upon arrival at Clark Air Base, the weather was pretty much as expected – hot and humid. A sign at the entrance to the base jungle school read, 'The College of Jungle Knowledge – Learn and Return.'

USAF personnel and local natives 'negritos' who lived in the jungles served as instructors. Initial training took place on the base where students were taught about the animals and vegetation they would come across, which ones to be aware of, and how to deal with them. Students were also taught how to get picked up by helicopter if that should become necessary, and how to descend from treetops if they were to ever parachute into such a situation. They were exposed to the different types of booby traps used by Viet Cong (VC) and regular North Vietnamese Army (NVA) to eliminate opposing forces. Instruction was also provided regarding methods to detect and avoid such traps.

From the base, they went to jungle areas accessible only by foot or by helicopter and observed firsthand the denseness of the foliage and how difficult, if not impossible, it was for helicopter crews to observe personnel in such areas needing their assistance. They were taught how to vector the helicopters to their locations, and how to get smoke from flares to penetrate the foliage and rise above treetops to aid rescue personnel in their efforts to find them.

They also received valuable instruction regarding the abilities of personnel native to the jungle environment. The students were given an hour to disappear into the wilds and hide from their native, jungle inhabitant instructors. The 'negritos' were then sent out to locate and bring them back. In short order, every student became a prisoner of the natives and returned to a central location.

The lesson: these people know their territory like you know your own home back in the States. They live there. Students wanted to know how they could possibly be seen through such foliage that they thought would keep them out of sight. Unwittingly, the students all left telltale signs not apparent to them, but quite apparent to the natives. The native instructors were also accustomed to the scents of the jungle and anything out of the ordinary was an immediate cause for suspicion. Their innate ability made it relatively easy to capture the Americans and those very same abilities also made it very difficult for Americans to find them.

Jungle training seemed to even have a sobering effect on Eric. His usual exuberant, full speed ahead, approach seemed to have diminished somewhat and Stan noticed a narrowing of his eyes, furrowing of his brow, and a steeliness about him that was not before apparent.

The night before their departure from "the world" as soldiers described everything outside of Vietnam, the course attendees compared notes, tried to raise spirits, and tried to learn as much as they could from each other before entering the 'real deal.'

Three

Fire

1

The scene was surreal as their aircraft approached Da Nang Air Base. It was dusk and the skies around the base lit up on occasion as the various types of ordinance utilized were interspersed with what appeared to be tracer rounds from aircraft not visible to the naked eye. Most of that activity was taking place west of the airfield. Dante's Inferno is what came to mind as Stan surveyed what was to become his new home for what now seemed like an eternity.

After deplaning, the group of very quiet new arrivals was herded into what looked like a cattle pen and awaited whatever was planned for them. A loud voice coming from behind the soldiers boomed, "Lieutenants Summers and Marks, report to me." Eric and Stan turned around and an imposing figure wearing an Air Force fatigue uniform bearing black markings indicating a rank of major appeared before them. They walked toward the major, snapped to attention, and saluted, saying, "Yes sir." The major did not return the salute. He just looked them over quickly and said, "Drop those salutes and follow me." They did as they were told, and entered a jeep behind the major. Major Bill Bannon introduced himself as their commanding officer and told them that they were now in a war zone and to never again salute another officer while there unless they intended to make that officer a target.

A very bumpy jeep ride took the trio over narrow, winding, dirt pathways until finally reaching paved roadway. They proceeded to what the major called the main compound and stopped in front of a building that was to serve as their quarters. It was a long narrow wooden structure with a hallway at its center and rooms along each side. Its exterior resembled a military barracks, and there was an entire row of such buildings. Sandbag piles had been arranged at various locations and the entire compound was enclosed with cyclone fencing.

They entered the building and followed the major down a narrow hallway. Unlike a typical barracks, it had been divided into individual dormitory-style rooms, each accommodating two personnel. Halfway down the hallway, they turned right into a community latrine area complete with shower facilities. Major Bannon then returned to the hallway, continued to the far end of the building, and opened a door at its right side. He ushered them inside the room, told them to get some sleep, and let them know that he would return for them later.

After looking around, Eric said, "Nice guy, huh?"

"Hmm. Look at this room, Eric. Remind you of anything?"

"Yeah, it does. Much like rooms at El Cid (The Citadel). About the same small size, two bunk beds, two desks with chairs, two lockers."

Stan replied, "Yeah, the only differences I see are no windows, there are flak jackets and helmets hanging at each end of the bunks and, damn, look at this, that's a window unit air conditioner in the wall and it is working."

They later found out that pilots were about the only personnel at the base provided with air-conditioned quarters.

Lieutenant Marks took the top bunk as was his habit during years at military school and Eric was only too happy to accommodate the request. When incoming shells strike the earth, debris from the exploding devices tend to spray in upward and outward directions which is exactly why soldiers are trained to 'hit the dirt' when made aware of incoming rounds. Da Nang was known by many as either "Rocket City" or "Rocket Alley" due to the frequency of attacks usually from high terrain west of the base, and usually during nighttime hours. The top bunk may not have been the best choice, but it was a done deal.

After what turned out to be nothing more than a brief nap, the door to their room flew open and Major Bannon said, "Okay, that's enough with the beauty sleep, let's go, we've got things to do."

The two lieutenants obeyed their orders and stood up. The major then completed the tour of the main compound showing them areas that included a small basketball court and a small gym supplied with equipment apparently familiar to the 'old man.'

The old man, Major Bannon, was probably in his late thirties and was obviously in top physical condition. After letting his new charges know that he expected them to keep in shape, he showed them additional areas such as a banking facility, chow hall, officers' club, barber shop, and a movie theater/assembly area for squadron briefings. They then went to a supply area where they were each issued two sets of fatigues and a pair of jungle boots. Stan and Eric were still wearing Class A uniforms and were not appropriately dressed for their new duties. The major also instructed them to leave a box of Tide, a can of spray starch, and the appropriate amount of piasters (local currency) on their bunks monthly for 'Momasan.'

"For who?" Stan said.

Major Bannon explained that it was a good deal. "Momasans provide maid service. Leave your used uniform hanging on your bunk every day and when you return, at the end of the day, it will have been cleaned and pressed." He told them about how much the piaster amount was equivalent to in U.S. dollars and both lieutenants agreed that it was indeed a good deal. They later observed that the 'Momasans' did much more than just clean uniforms. They also cleaned the billets, including the latrine areas and the shower facilities.

Finally, Major Bannon instructed the men to return to their 'hooch' (quarters), stow their Class A's, change uniforms, go to the chow hall for eats, and turn in. He instructed them to be at the chow hall again tomorrow morning at 0700 hours to have breakfast with him and others. His parting instruction was, "When leaving the chow hall, you'll see guys taking tablets from a bowl near the door. Take one of those tablets every day." After seeing quizzical expressions on their faces, he said, "Malaria."

Stan and Eric changed into their newly issued gear. In a decisive moment, they promised each other to always wear their 'dog tags' while 'in country.' They had not always been in the habit of wearing them and now thought it to be a good idea.

After checking out the chow hall and the officers' club, Stan sat down at his desk and penned a letter to Melanie while Eric hit the hay. He was tired, but could not sleep until he talked to Melanie. It was a one-way conversation, but he imagined her expressions and responses as he wrote. He pictured her intelligent, pretty face and wondered how his unborn child was progressing. Letters were the only means of communication between them and they were very much a lifeline. By the time one of his letters reached her and he received a response, two weeks might easily have passed and what they would be reading could be old news indeed. This of course was his first letter to Melanie since arriving in country and he wanted to sound as upbeat as possible. He informed her of his air-conditioned quarters and that he was rooming with Eric. The conditions were sanitary for a war zone and everything he needed was at hand. But what he really wanted other than to embrace Melanie was to know how she was feeling and that everything was okay at home. He expressed his love for them all and tried to get some sleep. After staring at the ceiling for what seemed a long time, he finally drifted off and dreamed of the life he was missing in what was now such a far off land known as America.

If mental telepathy is indeed a valid form of communication, these two were up there with Bell and Marconi and should have applied for patent rights. Melanie wrote a letter to her husband trying to do the same thing. She knew that he had enough on his mind and did not want to add to his burden. She told him that she was doing great and that the baby was behaving nicely. Melanie also told him that she had notified the appropriate personnel at Cannon Air Force Base regarding her status and that she expected to be discharged shortly. Mr. and Mrs. Blake asked her to express their love for him and she did so along with her own deep love and that of 'baby.'

Since their military college days, Lieutenants Marks and Summers had spent years of their relatively young lives rising early every morning to prepare for long, productive days. This was their first official day at a new assignment; it was important to them, and they wanted very much to make a good impression. They arrived at the chow hall at 0645 hours and waited on the chow line along with quite a few airmen and soldiers starting their day as well.

Da Nang Air Base housed members of all forces of the military and the airpower represented was much more than just that of the U.S. Air Force. Army, Navy, Marine personnel, as well as members of allied forces, were also present. VNAF (Vietnamese Air Force), ARVN (Army of the Republic of Vietnam), ROK (Republic of Korea), Canadian and Australian personnel among others were present on occasion.

At the chow line, Stan noticed that the Air Force sergeant just ahead of him had an interesting combination of food on his plate, and Stan asked the server to give him whatever it was he just gave to the sergeant. The sergeant looked over and said, "Never had SOS on scrambled eggs before, Lieutenant?"

"Can't say that I have, Sarge. Looks good though."

"It is, sir, take my word, you'll love it."

Eric looked at his buddy's plate and in a low voice said, "God damn, boy, you gonna eat that?"

They looked around for a place to sit and noticed that Major Bannon was already seated with a few others and that there were a couple of seats available for them. They approached the table and Major Bannon said, "So what took you two sleepy heads so long?"

"Thought we were supposed to meet at 0700 hours, sir." said Stan.

"Let's get this straight right now. Anytime I schedule something, all my pilots report thirty minutes prior for a briefing. Got that?"

"Yes sir."

The other three pilots present were captains and they smiled at the exchange. They introduced themselves to the newly arrived lieutenants and one of them said, "Don't worry guys, the old fart gets the discipline he wants because we love him, not because he barks."

"Hey, hey now," the major piped up. "Don't be spillin' my beans just yet, I'm not finished havin' my fun."

They all laughed and that broke the tension for the two new pilots. Stan said, "Look Eric, these guys are eating this stuff too."

Eric looked at the other plates and said, "Oh God, think I'm gonna be sick."

More laughter ensued, with statements such as, "This is a main staple around here," "Good stuff," and "Bet you'll be eating it before long."

Stan and Eric took an immediate liking to their new comrades and began to realize that the purpose of this meeting was simply to make introductions and first impressions. Turned out that the major was a decent guy after all.

During the meal, one of the captains quipped, "Hey Lieutenant, I think I know a VNAF (Vietnamese Air Force) lieutenant with a DEROS (Date of Estimated Return from Overseas) that is before yours." Again, everyone laughed except the two new arrivals. They responded with slight smiles.

After breakfast, Major Bannon, Stan, and Eric entered the major's jeep and he took them to their operations building at the air base flight line. He showed them around and saw to it that they were issued proper gear for operating the O-2 aircraft. Among the items were approach charts, standard instrument departure procedure charts, aerial charts, standard mesh survival vest with pockets for such things as flares, first aid kits, emergency radio, and spare batteries. Other items included flight helmets and flak jackets. They were also shown where to store their gear and were issued standard 38 caliber, Smith & Wesson, six shot revolvers along with M-16 rifles.

The men then proceeded to the flight line and the major gave his new guys a complete inspection tour of one of the 'Ducks' that would serve as their offices during their tour of duty. They were, of course, already checked out in its operation, but any local procedures developed and used for adaptation to local requirements needed to be reviewed. They were shown where to store their rifles aboard the aircraft. Gun racks were provided on the cockpit wall behind the pilot. The only way into or out of the cockpit was through the door located at the right side of the plane and the pilot sat at the left side. Parachutes were not provided since it was difficult to enter or exit the aircraft and they normally operated at low altitudes, too low for parachute deployment. In addition to that, the rear propeller blade was an additional hazard for exit by parachute.

Major Bannon showed them why it was wise to have two flak jackets in use while flying. They should wear one and place the other on their seats to help protect themselves from ground fire.

The men then returned to the operations building and reviewed information contained on a wall chart. It was a map of the area their unit was responsible to patrol. That area was primarily from just north of the air base to the DMZ (De-Militarized Zone).

Forward air controllers were required to fly low-level reconnaissance missions daily for the purpose of providing intelligence information. The FACs flew these missions routinely and it was their duty to become very familiar with the neighborhood. They needed to pay attention to any changes from day to day and to note that information. Observations of vehicle movement and or troop movement needed to be reported immediately via radio to tactical air control for possible interdiction, and they also monitored appropriate radio frequencies for information requiring their assistance. Enemy supply routes in the area were monitored closely by FACs and any activity reported was to be dealt with swiftly.

After the tour and briefing, Major Bannon instructed Stan and Eric to report to squadron operations at 0700 hours the following morning and to use the remainder of the day to review procedures described in the manuals and charts he provided.

The two newly assigned pilots utilized the time provided by their major wisely. They studied local air traffic procedure and thought of their old buddy Rich, the air traffic control officer at Laughlin Air Force Base. Rich made sure his friends took their business seriously and demanded that they adhere to established procedure. After reviewing the approach charts and departure procedures for the air base, Stan and Eric took note of the fact that they had access to two, long, parallel, runways oriented in a north/south direction and that the RAPCON and GCA units were located between those runways. The Gulf of Tonkin and The South China Sea were located just east of the air base and high terrain to its west. It was also noted that notices to airman (NOTAMs) identified an artillery fan fire area west and northwest of the airfield requiring pilots to remain at certain altitudes while operating in those areas.

According to briefings received from Major Bannon, they would usually patrol sectors north of Da Nang and west of the Gulf of Tonkin. The Ho Chi Minh Trail, which was by no means identifiable as a trail at all, primarily comprised the geography just described. North Vietnamese troops moved men and equipment in that area to supply forces operating within various sectors. Finding them and eliminating them was the job at hand. Lieutenant Marks thought about lessons learned during jungle survival training and the words of advice provided by Mr. Blake. *We may think of ourselves as the hunters in this environment, but unless we are very careful, we could very easily become the hunted.* Lieutenants Marks and Summers discussed and considered the information available to them and decided that they should keep a close eye on each other, especially during the initial phase of this tour, until they became more familiar and more comfortable with their duties.

Having learned their lesson the previous day regarding reporting to Major Bannon, they decided to arrive at the operations building no later than 0630 hours since they had been directed to report at 0700 hours. That meant a quick and light breakfast at the chow hall. They arrived at approximately 0630 hours and Major Bannon was already there. He greeted them by smiling and saying, "Glad to see you boys decided to show up on time today. Help yourselves to a cup of coffee."

The major reviewed his operational plan for the day with his new lieutenants, utilizing the same large wall chart from the day before, and told them that they would accompany him for an unspecified period of time for familiarization training. He intended to take them along the so called 'trail' north of the field and point out specific landmarks and areas he was particularly interested in regarding possible North Vietnamese activity. They would each be flying their own O-2 aircraft and communicate via a VHF radio frequency preselected as a channel on the radio equipment aboard their aircraft.

The major accompanied Stan and Eric to each of their airplanes individually and watched as they conducted their preflight inspections. He had them stow their gear, ensuring that they wore proper equipment and placed flak jackets on the seat of their planes. When all was ready, all three pilots dialed into the control tower ground control radio frequency and Major Bannon made the transmissions. Using his call sign, he notified ground control that he was a flight of three O-2s requesting taxi instructions to the active runway for takeoff. He received taxi clearance and began moving his aircraft, followed by Stan, while Eric took up the rear. Upon reaching the active runway, the three pilots taxied their aircraft into a run up area to check engine performance prior to requesting take off clearance.

When the two lieutenants were satisfied with their engine performance, they each reported on a discrete frequency to Major Bannon that they were ready for takeoff. All three pilots then changed to the tower controller's frequency and the major advised that a flight of three O-2s was ready to take position on the runway, as a flight, for individual takeoff rolls. They were cleared into position and were instructed to hold for takeoff clearance. Major Bannon took center position on the runway with Stan at his left rear and Eric at his right. The tower gave the flight takeoff clearance and the major rolled down the runway first. The O-2 doesn't need much runway to become airborne and as soon as Major Bannon's aircraft lifted off the runway, Stan started his take off roll. When Stan's aircraft lifted off the runway, Eric followed. They joined up in flight formation after clearing the departure end of the runway and the major told his flight to switch to a preselected radio channel.

As the formation proceeded northeast toward the coastline, the flight leader, Major Bannon, instructed his wingmen to keep a loose formation. The U.S. and its allied air forces had control of the skies at this point in the war and enemy aircraft were not a factor. Ground fire, however, was a factor and they were flying at low altitude.

This is exactly the type of flying that appealed to Lieutenant Marks. He loved to fly low and slow with time to enjoy viewing the terrain below and he marveled at the beauty of the Vietnamese countryside. It was so lush, so green, with beautiful waters and beaches east of them and gorgeous mountainous terrain to the west. *What a beautiful place for a vacation, if we ever stop blowing the place up,* he thought.

They continued following their flight leader for some time as the major pointed out certain landmarks and indicated to them where enemy activity had been previously spotted and dealt with. *It was spotted and dealt with and we are still reconnoitering the same area. How many times is it necessary to deal with the same problem before it's resolved?* Stan thought.

As they continued, Stan and Eric would occasionally look over at each other's aircraft. They had become the proverbial "comrades in arms" and they looked out for each other like brothers.

Major Bannon transmitted to them that he wanted to check out an area up ahead because he considered that sector suspicious. As they approached that location, the major pointed out a bend in the river ahead and to their left. He told them to remain at altitude while he descended to take a look. The lieutenants watched as Major Bannon descended to nearly treetop level for his observations of that location. He then climbed and rejoined the flight stating that he did not see anything unusual but had a bad feeling about that place.

Lieutenant Marks said, "Sir, want me to go down and take a look?"

"Negative" was the reply. "Go down once and you alert them as to your presence. Go back a second time and they may be ready for you. On the way back to base later, I may go down for another look."

The formation continued north and repeated this scenario a few more times before heading back south toward home. Stan loved his new aircraft; it responded to him beautifully, and he was becoming more comfortable in his office. He was an organized individual and had a predetermined place for everything and everything was in its place. With little more than a glance, he knew where it all was and he was able to reach and grab whatever he needed.

Lieutenant Marks was beginning to realize just how difficult it was to spot anything through the dense foliage and knew that he had to develop a trained eye. He intended to talk to the major about techniques necessary to accomplish that task, and he also needed a good pair of binoculars.

As they approached the initial area, where the major had descended for a previous look, he told them that he wanted to check it again more closely. While watching the major's aircraft, Lieutenant Marks thought, *I need to find out more about exactly what he is looking for down there.*

After rejoining the flight, the major announced, "Okay, let's get back to base."

The three pilots landed, parked their aircraft in designated areas, and rejoined in the operations building. Major Bannon asked, "Hey, you guys remember Tom, Dick, and Harry, right?" The three captains they had breakfast with the other day were conferring at a table after having returned from their scheduled missions. Stan and Eric looked at each other and Stan said, "Thomas, Richard, and Harold. Damn. Hey Eric, we work with Tom, Dick, and Harry." And they all laughed.

It was good to see that these guys work in such an informal atmosphere, thought Stan, *where rank is just part of the game.*

"How did it go up there?" Tom asked of the new guys.

Lieutenant Marks replied, "The major showed us some of the ropes today and we're trying to untangle them. How in the hell do you guys see anything down there? I didn't see much more than trees."

"And you won't," replied Harry. "Just try to remember what a place looked like the last time you saw it and decide if anything has changed. You'll start to develop a feeling about what is going on down there."

Stan paused before responding to Harry's statement. "Major Bannon had feelings about certain locations today and we watched as he checked them out."

"That's right," the major piped in. "And now I'll file my intelligence reports and see what the 'brain trusts' want to do, if anything." Gesturing toward Tom, Dick, and Harry, he continued, "That's what these guys are doing now and what you'll be doing when your feet are wet enough. I want you two to read these reports when we're finished with them. They will help you get a better feel for what we're looking at."

"Speaking of looking at," said Stan, "don't you guys use binoculars?"

"Oh yeah, over there, that locker over there," the major directed. "Store them with the rest of your gear."

2

Rocket attacks usually occurred during hours of darkness while many personnel were asleep and when 'Charlie' (North Vietnamese forces) could better operate undetected from the high terrain west of the base. The equipment they used was not very accurate and apparently just aimed in the general direction of the large, sprawling air base. It appeared that they launched these projectiles in great haste since they usually launched no more than six or so at about the same time and evidently departed rapidly to avoid detection. It had been Stan and Eric's experience thus far that all 'Charlie' had been able to do was to wake up a lot of people and plant some new craters in the ground. The flak jackets and helmets that hung from their bunks were never used because by the time they realized what was happening, it was all over.

Lieutenant Marks recalled hearing about an airman who dove from his bunk, in the dark, during such an attack and got a foot caught in a rotating fan. The foot was messed up a bit and the airman reported to a base medical facility to have it cleaned up and bandaged. As the story goes, that airman was awarded a purple heart for injuries sustained as a result of enemy activity. That made Stan smile and it also made him thankful that he had an air-conditioned billet and did not have to rely on a fan.

Their flying routine went on for a couple of weeks and the two 'newbies' were becoming very accustomed to their daily assignments. One day, during a morning briefing, the major instructed Lieutenants Marks and Summers to accompany him on a 'frag order' (fragmentary order) response. The 'brain trust' that Major Bannon referred to earlier decided that an area reported as suspicious a number of times by FACs should be attacked. The major explained that during one of his treetop descents, he believed he observed a single truck hidden near foliage. Where there was one, there were likely to be many more. Enemy convoys were known to hide during daytime hours when they could be spotted from the air and to make their movements during hours of darkness.

The usual flight of three O-2s departed Da Nang and proceeded to the first location the major had descended to when he took them on their initial flight orientation. On the UHF frequency they were monitoring, a flight of two F-4's out of Da Nang, using fighter squadron call signs, checked in with them and the major responded. On their VHF radios, the major told his flight members to remain clear while he marked the area designated for attack. Major Bannon descended his aircraft and fired off a number of 'Willie Petes.' Huge, white, smoke billows appeared in the distance and an F-4 pilot reported the target area in sight.

Major Bannon instructed his flight to remain clear of the target area, and to remain west of it, since the F-4s were approaching from the southeast and the wind was blowing the smoke toward the northeast. He then rejoined his flight and they watched as the jet pilots released napalm canisters on the target area. The jets continued in a northwest direction and upon impact, the igniting napalm spread across an enormous area appearing to completely engulf anything and everything in its path. Flames emitted as a result of the attack created a massive expanse of red, orange, and yellow hellfire. The destruction was devastating to behold.

That mission complete, they continued routine reconnaissance. To a seasoned FAC, this was just another day at the office. But Stan was still a rookie, not yet a seasoned veteran by any stretch of the imagination. His observations left him deep in thought and presented questions he was not prepared to answer.

Melanie's letters to her husband kept him informed of 'baby's' progress and all appeared to be well. She seemed to be in good spirits, at home in Abilene with her parents, and had been discharged from the Air Force. Stan's allotment checks were being deposited in their joint account, and she asked about the U.S. government savings bonds she had been receiving. When Stan wrote back, he explained that he had established an allotment for savings bonds and asked her to secure them in a safe place as an education fund for 'baby.'

Her letters were always upbeat and encouraging, filled with anticipation for parenthood and the future. In their correspondence, they discussed names for the baby and agreed on Adam for a boy and Amelia for a girl. Melanie wanted to keep her husband's spirits as high as possible. She admired and respected him, and very much believed that he was doing the right thing for his country. But she also loved him very much and was desperately concerned for his safety.

Stan often thought about the baby and the fact that he would not be able to hold him until the child was about six months old. Missing out on the wonders of watching his newborn grow up had been gnawing at him.

After much contemplation, Lieutenant Marks no longer believed that he would make the Air Force his career. He wasn't sure of the direction he would take after leaving the service as yet and did not want to discuss the subject with anyone but Melanie. He decided to do that in Hawaii.

Although Stan occasionally questioned the wisdom of missions assigned to him, he also questioned his own ability to judge decisions made by his leaders. However, he was absolutely sure that he must perform his duty to the best of his ability and that he would never disappoint his brothers in arms. His mission, as he now saw it, was to help as many of his fellow soldiers as possible return home safely, and he intended to include himself in that number. What kept him going were thoughts of the imminent birth of his child and joining his young bride during his R&R in Hawaii.

And boy, was he ever happy to have his good buddy Eric along with him. They established a routine when off duty to keep in shape by working out in the small gym equipped with a universal weight lifting apparatus and by jogging around the main compound after their workouts. Evenings were often spent having a few drinks at the officers' club with the rest of their crew discussing aviation, missions, and news from home.

Meals were available at the officers' club as well as at the chow hall. One evening, while Stan and Eric were at a table sharing a meal, Stan noticed a familiar figure enter the chow line and he exclaimed, "Hey Eric, look at that. Do you see what I see?"

Eric looked up and said, "Damn, no, is that really Rich?"

They both stood up, ran to their old buddy, and grabbed him good-naturedly before embracing. "Rich, what the hell are you doing here?" Eric asked.

Rich responded with a broad smile. "Let me get some chow and I'll let you know. I'll be right over to your table."

Stan and Eric were amazed that they were again together with their old friend Rich. This unexpected reunion did wonders for their spirits and the idea that their old air traffic control partner and former college classmate was back among them brightened their outlook.

Rich joined them and explained that he did not want to spend forever in Del Rio. He sent in 'dream sheets' (requests for transfer) repeatedly for a European assignment but never heard a word in response. When he learned that Stan and Eric had been deployed to Da Nang, he sent in another 'dream sheet' listing three bases in Vietnam, and his first choice was approved. He was now a crew chief at the Da Nang RAPCON (Radar Approach Control) facility and the three musketeers were back in action. After leaving the club, they walked back to their hooch and were surprised to find out that Rich had been billeted down the hall from them. Rich's superior officer was also a rated pilot and he secured air-conditioned quarters for his junior officers.

Stan and Eric's spirits were now higher than ever and whenever possible, Rich was included in their off-duty routine. Rich, however, was working rotating shifts at his 24 hour a day, seven day a week operation, so it wasn't as often as they would have liked.

Thanks to Rich, his old buddies were able to tour the air traffic control facilities at the air base. The RAPCON and GCA air traffic control units located between the two runways were somewhat reminiscent of the facilities back at Laughlin with notable exceptions. The entire facility made up a small compound. It was surrounded by metal revetments filled with sand to withstand blasts from rocket attacks and aircraft mishaps. Additional sandbags were placed in other locations around the area for controllers to respond to in the event of ground attack. M-16s were kept within the RAPCON for such an event and controllers were called into a briefing trailer on occasion for weapons handling training. Rich wanted to ensure that the controllers were able to load and utilize the weapons available to them during both day and nighttime situations. He was concerned they would not necessarily have the benefit of good lighting.

In addition to the large mobile RAPCON trailer was a smaller mobile unit for GCAs (Ground Controlled Approaches) and it was situated on a turntable. When the runway flow changed due to wind conditions, the tower supervisor notified the RAPCON supervisor, and controllers from within the unit went outside and manually pushed the unit on the turntable and then quickly realigned their radar scopes for use at the opposite end of the runways.

A trailer was located in the compound that served as an area for crew briefings prior to shift change, office area for crew chiefs, and storage for tape recording equipment. All transmissions and landline communications were recorded at that location. Rich explained that the tapes were routinely reviewed by controllers along with their supervisors to improve upon facility performance. The tapes were stored for that purpose and for review in the event of accident or incident.

There was also an outhouse located in the compound and that was the latrine facility for controllers while on duty. It was a wooden structure with a carving of a broadly smiling Snoopy mascot mounted on the roof. Snoopy was wearing his World War I fighter pilot goggles and leather helmet, with his red scarf trailing in the breeze, while flying his imaginary biplane atop his dog house. Rich opened the door to the building and a stench became immediately evident. Flies were buzzing about the place and it seemed to rattle every time a jet rolled by on the runways adjacent to the facility. Rich explained that the final duty of the mid shift ending at 0700 hours was to hook onto an open metal drum, from the rear of the structure, located beneath the seat inside the building and drag it out. They would then replace the drum with another, pour a flammable liquid into the old barrel, and light a fire. As the day watch crew drove their truck across the runway and toward the facility, they could observe the dark smoke emitted from within the compound.

A fairly large pile of sandbags was located at one end of the enclosed area and Rich explained it was a bunker built by the controllers for rocket attacks. Airmen located outside of the trailers, such as maintenance personnel and controllers moving from one trailer to another, would dive into that shelter in the event of attack.

In another area, not too far from that compound, was a unit called a Morest Crew manned by Marines. The runways at Da Nang were often wet and slippery due to monsoon conditions prevalent in that area. As a result of that and other conditions, jet aircraft returning to the base would often need the services of this unit. The wet runways became slippery and the aircraft would occasionally return with hung ordinance, meaning that the ordinance (bombs) did not deploy as intended and remained with the aircraft. Pilots returning to the field under such circumstances relayed pertinent information to approach controllers, including the weight of their aircraft and the speed at which they intended to engage a barrier. An assistant controller would then relay that information to the Morest Crew. Those soldiers would then erect a cable across the runway and adjust its tension according to information provided. Upon landing, the pilots would engage that cable to restrain their aircraft. Much like aircraft carrier operations, the cable would then be released for the pilots to taxi clear of the runway.

These Marines worked with equipment in close proximity to the runways in use and occasionally suffered injury and loss of life as a result of mishaps. Airmen staffing the air traffic control facilities, also located between the runways, were in a similar predicament and a klaxon horn was provided to be activated by the control tower when dangerous conditions in the vicinity of the radar units were observed. The intent was to alert personnel to evacuate the facilities; however, given the speed at which such events occurred, remaining at one's duty location was more often than not the best course of action.

Monsoon rains presented additional challenges to flight crews due to runway conditions, low ceilings, and reduced visibility. Stan and Eric were grateful to Rich for providing them with valuable information. While inside the RAPCON, they began to appreciate the conditions under which these controllers operated. Their equipment was dated; radio and radar equipment were in need of constant attention and repair, and the activity level due to the traffic volume handled was extraordinary.

Rich took time to carefully explain pitfalls of operating in the Da Nang area. He pointed out the artillery fan fire areas on the radar scopes that were to be avoided by aircraft flying at low altitudes. Artillery units operating in those areas would forward information to air traffic control regarding altitudes, coordinates, and duration of artillery strikes. The controllers would then record that information and keep aircraft clear of those areas.

Rich particularly emphasized the importance of lost communication procedures in the area. Using a radar scope, he showed them an aircraft that had been inbound from the north and was on a radar controlled dog leg to a final approach. That pilot was in the soup, meaning unable to see very far due to weather conditions. Many radio failures were experienced in those days and this 'lost comm' procedure was of extreme importance. Not far to the west of that aircraft's location was high terrain not visible to the pilot and the aircraft was flying at an altitude below the height of the terrain. If that pilot were to become unable to receive further communication from the controller, it was incumbent upon him to monitor his instruments closely. After crossing a radial emitted from a ground based navigational aid, it was necessary for the pilot to turn his aircraft inbound to the airport to avoid impact with that terrain. Unfortunately, aircraft had flown into those mountains before.

3

Stan and Eric had begun to patrol areas assigned to them for surveillance individually and were able to communicate by radio with each other, with other FACs, and with other facilities. They had arrived at Da Nang at the end of a dry weather period and were now into a monsoon or rainy season. By Stan's calculations, 'baby' would arrive at the end of this period of almost continuous rain and he would be joining Melanie in Hawaii at its termination.

Reconnaissance flights had become routine and rather frustrating since detection of enemy activity had become even more difficult due to weather conditions. Reports filed by the FACs provided little information and Stan was feeling a bit like ole Sergeant Schultz of Hogan's Heroes fame: "I see nuttink, I hear nuttink, I know nuttink."

One day, Major Bannon took his entire group on a tour of the morgue located at the base. He told them that he wanted them to observe the reason why they were there. Stan's ears perked up. He was about to finally get an answer to this question. While looking around the morbid facility, the major said, "Look guys, let's all take a good look. These guys were, and a lot more out there right now are, counting on us. We've got a job to do and that job is not to just file meaningless reports after every mission. I know it's hard, but that is why we are here. We are here to do the hard work it takes to help save these poor guys. Our job is to locate the enemy and eliminate them before they can do this to us. We all want to go home. Well, so did they and there are many more out there praying for that opportunity. Now, it's up to us to figure out how we are going to get that job done."

That was what he had been waiting to hear. This seemed to have an impact on the group and it did have an impact on Stan. This short excursion into morbid reality reinforced his views regarding mission objectives. He thought about Bart Small. He was out there somewhere right now and he also thought about his brother, Pat, about to graduate from military college and enter the Marine Corps. *The major is right,* he thought, *but what are we to do?*

The solution turned out to be obvious. There was no other choice. Due to weather conditions, they were forced to continue reconnaissance missions at lower attitudes. 'Charlie' did not stop his movement of supplies because he got wet. Our ground troops were still making contact with their forces and they seemed to be supplied better than ever. Rocket attacks at the air base were now more frequent as evidenced by an aviation fuel tank that had been burning day and night for two days.

The FACs had been flying at close to treetop level for some time now with little success as far as making observations; however, some had success in drawing occasional ground fire. That was what the FACs needed. They needed 'Charlie' to give himself away by firing on their aircraft. This was of course very risky, but when it worked, the FACs gained altitude, notified ground operations of the contact, and awaited information regarding whether or not strike aircraft were available to respond.

Stan returned to base one day, stowed his gear, and filed his reports after a rather uneventful day of playing 'clay pigeon' for 'Charlie.' A couple of the other pilots were already there and they all went about their business routinely. After a while, everyone reported in except Eric and someone said, "Hey Stan, where's Eric?"

He looked up and said, "I don't know. I haven't seen him yet."

Major Bannon looked at the guys, realized that no one had heard from Eric, and immediately went to call him on their standard operations frequency. There was no response and, suddenly, everyone became more alert. Eric was the only pilot that had not returned to base. Major Bannon went to the wall chart in the briefing room and called everyone over. He pointed out Eric's assigned area for that day and asked them when anyone last had contact with him. They all looked at each other and realized they had a situation on their hands. One of their number had gone missing and they knew that under current weather conditions and with darkness approaching, unless he returned soon, he would not be found that day.

Stan knew Eric better than anyone there. He thought about him at college, his performance in flight training, on water skies, and on motorcycles. Eric was devoted to duty and he was a daredevil. Had all that low-level flying caught up with him? Did he spot something and then return to the same location for a second look? Stan did not put that past him and was now extremely worried. He did not go to the wall chart with the others; he remained sitting there deep in thought, staring into space. Major Bannon took note and waved the guys over toward his young lieutenant. Without singling him out, he announced, okay guys, here is what we are going to do. I know it's early, and Eric might still return today, but I'm going to notify search and rescue right now for the possibility of a downed O-2 in Eric's sector. And if he is not retrieved today, at first light tomorrow we are all going to divide up Eric's assigned sector and conduct our own search.

Stan looked up and nodded to the major in a thankful manner. He was not happy with the prospect of Eric being out there all night, but he did not know what else could be done. As much as he wanted to go out there right now, he was fully aware of the futility of that action. Hell, they'll all be lucky to find anything tomorrow.

Meanwhile, Eric was scrambling around jungle vegetation attempting to keep body and soul intact. He had taken ground fire, including what he believed to be a hit at the rear of his aircraft from a shoulder-fired projectile. It was all he could do to crash land his aircraft in some sort of controlled fashion without sustaining serious injury to himself. The aircraft came to final rest after a violent impact and Eric was amazed that he had been able to survive at all. But he knew he had to get out of his 'Duck' and that was no easy task. The plane was severely mangled and he had to maneuver his body through wreckage and get to the right side of his aircraft since exit was not possible from where he had been seated at the left side. This had to be accomplished as quickly as possible since 'Charlie' would probably be on top of him shortly. He grabbed his M-16 rifle from the cockpit rack behind him and used its butt end to push debris away. Eric did finally manage to pull himself free from the debris and was outside the aircraft when he thought he heard something in the distance.

Fortunately, Eric crashed at the opposite side of a body of water from the area where he had been initially hit and that hindered the ability of 'Charlie' to reach him. His jungle survival training instincts kicked in and he moved as best he could away from the aircraft. It was then that Eric realized he had sustained injuries. He wiped his brow and his hand and sleeve became red with blood. Eric limped severely as he tried to run, but could only manage fairly slow movements due to pain from yet undetermined injuries.

Eric got as far as he could from the aircraft and hid in what appeared to be good cover at the edge of a fairly large clearing. It was starting to get dark and he thought of darkness as a friend, since he believed it would help him evade detection. He had not been able to transmit any information regarding his location prior to crash landing because he had been hit at such low altitude and time did not permit anything but attempts to control his plane and to then quickly escape the wreckage.

After taking stock of his situation, he realized that in addition to his M-16, he did have a flare gun, an emergency radio, and a first aid kit, in his survival vest. He was also carrying a side arm. Stopping the bleeding from his head was his immediate concern and he used his first aid kit to tend to that wound. He took some solace in the fact that his aircraft was equipped with an emergency locator transmitter (ELT). Upon impact, the transmitter was designed to emit signals on emergency frequencies allowing search and rescue personnel to find him, and he prayed that the thing was working. The transmitter was supposed to be good for 24 to 48 hours.

Back at the base, Stan's mental state could best be described as horribly depressed. He felt guilty for not being out there right now looking for his long-time, dear friend. Eric had become his best friend and they looked out for each other like brothers.

Stan was returning to his hooch, lost in his thoughts and looking at the ground, when he literally bumped into Rich. He looked up at his friend and the look in his eyes indicated that something was terribly wrong. Rich put an arm around his pal, led him to his room, and guided him to a chair. The mini-fridge in that room was always stocked with beer. Rich immediately popped a can and handed it to his friend. Stan was obviously distraught and, holding the beer can, just stared off into space.

Rich finally said, "Damn it, Stan, are you going to tell me what's going on or am I gonna have to smack the crap out of you?"

"Eric's missing," he blurted.

The look on Rich's face became one of alarm. "What?" he asked.

"He's missing. He didn't return today. Search and rescue is out looking for him,"

Rich tried his best to sound confident. "Well, you know crazy Eric. He'll turn up soon. He always pulls through somehow. He'll get through this."

Stan took a long swig of his beer and sat quietly with Rich as they tried not to envision the worst possible outcome. The troubled pilot shook his head, stood up, and silently walked to his room. Entering the room and looking around, everything reminded him of Eric. The exhausted aviator then crashed onto his bunk and immediately fell asleep.

Sometime later, he was awakened by what he thought was Eric's voice telling him to get his dead ass out of bed. He looked around and tried to shake off the fog and dizziness brought on by his temporary venture into netherworld. As his spirit began to slowly re-enter his body, he saw Eric standing before him.

Stan asked, "What the hell happened to you, you son-of-a-bitch?"

A voice responded, "What?"

After rubbing his eyes, he looked again and realized it was Major Bannon standing before him.

He mumbled, "Oh, sorry sir, I thought it was Eric."

"Well, in a way it is. Eric is back. The medics are taking care of him; he's a bit banged up."

Stan jumped to the floor from his top bunk and said, "What! He's alive?"

"You bet your sweet 'bippy' he is. Now let's get over there and see him."

The overjoyed lieutenant threw his arms around his major and started to cheer. His cheering was loud, tears of joy came rolling down his face, and he began slapping the major's back as he thanked him for saving his friend.

"Will you cut this crap out and get your damn self under control boy? Let's go see Eric."

By this time, the noise had aroused the curiosity of others in the building and Rich was standing at the doorway. After bestowing upon Rich, treatment similar to that he had just dealt to his commanding officer, he introduced them and they all headed off to the medical facility.

On the way, Major Bannon explained that a Jolly Green rescue helicopter, dispatched to the area for search and rescue, picked up Eric's ELT signal and proceeded to that location. Apparently Eric heard the approaching helicopter and fired his flare gun to help the airborne pilots find him. The chopper crew encountered ground fire and A-1 Skyraiders accompanying the Jolly Green strafed the enemy position to provide necessary cover for the rescue.

When they reached the medical facility, they learned that Eric's condition was stable, but that he was sedated and asleep. He sustained multiple fractures to ribs, a hip, possible concussion, and loss of blood. Although they were unable to speak with Eric, they were thrilled to see that he had survived and was being properly cared for. They were informed that Eric would not be returning to flight status any time soon and that, when possible, he would be transferred out of country for better care. Lieutenant Marks requested that he be notified if Eric was able to have visitors before he was transferred out and was told that their commander would be advised in that event.

With smiles on their faces, the three men left the medical facility and headed to the officers' club. What had been a horrific day turned into cause for some celebration and toasts to a comrade's survival. The celebration went on into the early morning hours as pilots from other squadrons joined in the celebration. Rescue of a fellow airman warmed the hearts of all present. Every one of them knew that it could have been them needing such assistance and they drank not only to Eric and his rescuers, but to the gods that watch over them as well. Drinks flowed and in a highly inebriated state, they physically supported each other's ability to remain vertical as they laughingly staggered into the hooch where Stan crashed after the major boosted him into the upper rack. Major Bannon then crashed in Eric's lower bunk.

That was all, of course, highly irregular.

Stan's correspondence with Melanie was prolific. They wrote to each other regularly and he was kept up to date on the progress of 'baby.' It was almost time now, and before long, he would be able to join Melanie in Hawaii. He remained positive in his letters home and did not make any mention of the ordeal with Eric. Melanie was about to give birth and he did not want to cause any unnecessary anxiety. He tried to describe tales of his daily exploits as boring and uneventful, and sometimes they were boring indeed. *Good Lord, please bore me more often,* he would occasionally think.

Time and time again Lieutenant Marks would really wonder why all these American soldiers were over there 'helping' these people. He was once walking along a dirt roadway on base when a VNAF airman, approaching from the opposite direction on a motorbike, grabbed the wristwatch he was wearing on his right arm. The watch had a stretch band and the guy tried to yank it off his arm. Stan made a tight fist with his right hand and yanked it hard toward his left shoulder. The bike rider let go, the watch remained on his wrist, and the cyclist nearly lost control of the machine as it veered erratically away. The motorbike was as common a mode of transportation to Vietnamese soldiers as cars were to American soldiers back in the states. The damn things were always zipping around all over the place which is why American personnel often and disparagingly referred to the riders as "Zips."

Another time, he was sitting in the back of a fully loaded jeep that was moving slowly on the base when a VNAF airman ran up to him attempting to grab the aviator sunglasses he was wearing off his face. He lashed out and punched the guy in the face with his right hand while he held onto the glasses with his left.

Damn! Stan thought to himself. *Is this some kind of a friggin' joke? What the hell am I doing here? These people are supposed to be our allies and we are supposed to be helping them. Do they really want our help? Are they really our allies? Really?*

Then he thought about the first time he went to get a haircut in the main compound shop. He was surprised to see that the barber was a Vietnamese in civilian attire and did not appear very friendly. Stan and the barber were the only two people there; no smiles or words were exchanged. Sometime during the middle of the haircut, the guy placed one hand on Stan's chin and the other on the back of his head. With a quick yank, he twisted his head and he heard the sound of a 'crack.' Stan was startled and his reaction was one of alarm. *Was this guy trying to do me in?* When he left the place, he told another American officer what happened and he was told they do that all the time. It was supposed to be some kind of relaxation technique. *Relaxation hell,* he thought. *I won't be relaxed till I get on that 'Freedom Bird'* (the flight back to the States).

He had a difficult time thinking of Vietnamese people as his friends. The cultures were so very different; he did not understand them at all. They did not smile and they were not friendly. If they wanted his help, they certainly did not express it, and there was certainly no indication of gratitude that he was able to discern. If anything, he detected a resentment toward his presence and Stan did not want to be anywhere he was not wanted. Every time he approached a Vietnamese while he was there, all he encountered was an expressionless stare that seemed to be yelling at him and saying in no uncertain terms, "Get the hell out of here and stay out."

Eric did recover to a point where he was able to receive visitors for brief periods, but he was still under the influence of drugs to keep pain under control. Upon hearing this, Stan raced over to the infirmary to see him before he was shipped out. Eric was groggy, but his eyes were open and he managed to smile when he saw his friend.

The first thing Stan said was, "I'm sorry, Eric. I'm really sorry, please forgive me."

Eric just looked at him, as he gradually became awake, and said, "Huh?"

"You needed me, Eric, and I wasn't there for you."

With a halting and muffled speech pattern, Eric said, "Believe me, you didn't want to be there. I'm a stupid ass. That should never have happened. I was there too long and was asking for it. Of course, I did my job and I did find the bastards." He laughed softly.

"Thanks pal, I needed to hear that. They tell me you are going to be okay and that you will be going home soon…you lucky devil." In reality, he would be taken to a military medical facility back in 'the world' for additional care before decisions could be made regarding his future.

"Yeah, that's what they tell me too, but I don't feel good about leaving you guys behind."

As they were speaking, Rich walked into the room. The three friends reminisced about their adventures on the boat on Lake Amistad in Texas and about the crazy stunts Eric would pull.

"Yeah, they were good times," Eric said. "We'll have to get together somewhere back home when this is all over, okay?"

"Hell yeah," said Stan. Before long, the major joined them, along with Tom, Dick, and Harry. They all complimented Eric on his survival skills and wished him well. Eric, the lucky guy, was alive and he was going home. His buddies did much to boost the spirits of their stricken comrade and they improved their own morale as a result.

After leaving the medical facility, Stan gathered together his roommate's personal effects, which didn't amount to much, and had them shipped to his home of record, his parents' home in Florida. With Eric gone, he was starting to spend more time with Rich, but it also gave him more time alone until Eric's replacement arrived.

4

Monsoon season added to some downtime for Stan, but not for Rich. Duty at the RAPCON (Radar Approach Control) unit became more intense as their services were needed more than ever by fighter pilots, cargo pilots, troop transports, and others. Stan's operations generally required decent visibility, while many others continued missions during IFR (Instrument Flight Rule) conditions. Bad weather or instrument conditions required that air traffic controllers provide separation between aircraft, when pilots are not able to see other planes, as they proceed to and from the airbase and to and from their mission areas.

While having dinner together at the officers' club one evening, Rich told Stan about something unnerving that occurred that morning and unnerving may have been putting it mildly. Rich met his entire crew at the chow hall that morning for a great breakfast of SOS on scrambled eggs, toast, and coffee. He had a very high regard for the work his men did and wanted to let them know just how much he appreciated their efforts. Rich was the crew chief and the only officer of the bunch. At twenty-five years old, he was the oldest member of the crew except for his top sergeant, an old man of about thirty-two.

After a good breakfast, the crew boarded their truck for the ride out to the RAPCON. The sergeant drove the truck and Rich sat in the passenger seat. There was room for only two people in the cab of the truck and the rest of the crew sat on benches situated along its sides at the rear. Visibility that morning was extremely poor due to drizzle and fog. The RAPCON was located between two parallel runways at the base requiring that they drive across one of the runways to reach the radar unit. The vehicle was equipped with a radio enabling them to contact the control tower for clearance to cross the runway.

As they approached the runway, they could barely see across its width due to the weather conditions. The sergeant had been thoroughly enjoying a humorous story he was telling his young lieutenant. He stopped the truck, picked up the radio transmitter, and contacted the control tower for permission to cross the runway. A garbled transmission was received from the tower and the sergeant proceeded forward across the runway as he continued with his story. Rich did not understand the tower's radio transmission, but he did not question the more experienced sergeant. As they approached the center of the runway, they began to hear a ferocious roar that was getting progressively louder. Stan noticed bright lights approaching the right side of the truck and heard a tremendous roar as an F-4 Phantom fighter jet lifted off the runway and flew directly overhead.

He hated to estimate how far above the truck the aircraft was, but it did not miss colliding with the truck by much. The vehicle shook and so did its occupants. The sergeant stopped telling his story and Rich did not say a word.

When they reached the briefing trailer Rich took note of the sober expressions on the faces of his crew members. The phone in the briefing trailer was ringing and Rich answered. The control tower chief was calling to check on the status of the crew. Rich told him that everyone was okay and that he would talk to him about it later.

Rich explained that he was known for being a stickler for detail and following procedure. As a result of this experience, he apologized to the entire crew during the morning briefing and later had a rather long, private, chat with his sergeant.

Relaying this story to his friend during dinner gave him what he thought was a good excuse for ordering rather stiff drinks, as if they ever needed an excuse anyway.

While alone in his room, Stan realized, *It's now me, myself, and I for the time being,* and the three roommates conversed regularly. Of course, Rich was still available to him, but he was down the hall, had a roommate, and worked strange rotating hours that he could never keep straight. This left Stan with plenty of time to write letters to not only Melanie, but to his brother Pat, his parents, and occasionally to other friends and relatives.

He received a 'care package' from an old friend of the family in New Jersey. The lady who sent the package was an elderly Italian immigrant his mother had befriended years ago and she included a message in the package written in her own hand. It said, 'I pray for you and I know that you are in God's hands.' Stan was touched by the sentiment and when he dug through the package was pleasantly surprised. It contained delicacies he had not seen or even thought about in years. He was delighted to find Italian cheese, salami, olives, bread sticks, and in the center of the carefully wrapped package was a mason jar containing a dark liquid. He looked and wondered, *What in the world is this?* After opening the jar, he sniffed it, tasted it, and laughed his tail off. That nice old lady knew

161

exactly what to send a soldier secluded in a war zone. It was a very strong blackberry brandy.

Stan decided to plan a small party in his room when he could arrange it with Rich and his roommate, Don. Rich was a Southern boy and Don was from the Midwest. As it turned out, neither of them had ever tasted such food and were surprised at the sharpness of the cheese, the spiciness of the salami, and the tastiness of the cured olives. The biggest hit, of course, was the brandy that was polished off in no time flat.

While writing a letter very late one evening, 'Charlie' paid another visit. Explosions interrupted Stan's train of thought, but by this time had become 'old hat.' He remained at his desk writing when an unusually loud explosion occurred, shaking his hooch. However, he thought no more about it after the vibrations subsided and he finished writing the letter.

The next morning during breakfast, Rich's roommate Don asked, "Hear what happened last night?"

Stan replied, "Yeah, little loud, wasn't it?"

Don continued with a look of concern, although somewhat detached. "More than loud, Stan. They hit a barracks in another compound and totally destroyed it. A barracks right next to it was also damaged. Worst part is that some aircraft mechanics were killed and others were wounded."

It's a war zone, thought Lieutenant Marks. *When your time is up, it's up.* He had been conditioned to such thoughts by his years at The Citadel as well as by his Air Force training. He thought about nights at college after 'All in Check.' Every evening they were confined to their rooms for a study period after which lights were extinguished and a room-to-room check was made to ensure that all cadets were in their bunks for the evening. Whenever a graduate had been killed in the war, a loudspeaker announcement was made while the cadets were lying in their bunks. They were informed of the former cadet's death including the name, rank, branch of service, class year graduated, and the circumstances surrounding his demise. Following the announcement, buglers played echo taps across the campus sending shrills up his spine and causing tears to well up in his eyes. That was the Corps' way of honoring its graduates who made the supreme sacrifice. It was also its way of saying "good night" to its current crop of cadets.

He sometimes thought, *I wonder if all of this will make sense to me someday. Those that sent me here must know what they are doing. Don't they? Is it ever time to question leadership? Do I have a right to ever question leadership?*

'Baby' was due to arrive on September 20 and he was planning to meet Melanie in early November for R&R in Hawaii. Time for all of this was quickly approaching and if the phrase has any meaning at all, he felt the 'ants in his pants.'

Nights at the officers' club with buddies were getting very old. They drank to excess and were entertained by Asian performers from who knew where. He thought that if he heard someone singing 'Wolling Dwown Dee Weeber' one more time, he would scream and on occasion believed that was exactly what happened to others displaying somewhat insane behavior.

The F-4 fighter squadron pilots appeared to be an unusually rowdy bunch, but Stan did not blame them for their behavior and apparently no one else did either. It had all become life under circumstances the U.S. was currently demanding of its warriors. Why weren't these guys in a chapel praying, or in their quarters reading good books to improve their minds, or in a gym improving their bodies? Far from it…they were busy arranging tables together end to end and sloshing beer all over them. They were preparing their runway to shoot GCAs. One at a time they would run across the room toward one end of the table and wearing their flight suits, belly wop onto the table and slide toward its far end. The pilot getting closest to the end of the fantasy runway without falling off won. Won what you ask? Why a pitcher of beer of course. What else? The club had become their church and this was their way of praying together. They were praying that tomorrow evening they would all still be there together to repeat this evening's splendid performance.

Rich, Stan, and Don compared notes on several occasions. They all worked in close proximity to the runway environment and were aware of the incredibly large number of flights being handled at the airfield. A navy aircraft carrier was stationed off the coast, east of Da Nang, and their pilots would occasionally come into the air base to refuel due to low and emergency fuel conditions. Rich and Don would relate to Stan that it was common for air traffic controllers to transmit phrases when receiving reports from pilots regarding a low fuel status such as, "Roger, number three reporting low fuel; report emergency fuel." The volume of traffic being handled was enormous resulting in delays to pilots awaiting takeoff and landing.

Most of those flights were leaving the base with ordinance and returning without very much of it. Some aircraft were loaded with the defoliant known as 'Agent Orange' utilized to eliminate obstructions to the vision of pilots, such as Stan, enabling them to identify enemy activity on the ground. The 'Agent Orange' substance, produced by a premier chemical company, was called such because its containers had a distinctive orange band around them making it identifiable to its handlers. American soldiers and the Vietnamese population were informed that the chemical was harmless and only eliminated foliage from trees. It appeared to Stan that no one ever questioned the accuracy of these claims.

Da Nang was only one of three large U.S. operated air bases in South Vietnam and there were many other such smaller facilities scattered throughout the country. Ordinance, chemicals, and all sorts of equipment were arriving and departing these airfields daily and this had been going on now for years. Where did all of this come from? What were the sources of these supplies? Who was paying for it? Who was profiting from all this?

Stan had so many questions. But, he didn't feel comfortable asking such questions because he felt guilty even thinking about them.

Enlisted personnel performing relatively unskilled functions appeared to be disproportionately men of color or of poor white background, while technically skilled personnel and officers seemed to be generally white men of middle class status. Wealth was only apparent to Stan in its ability to provide supplies for the conduct of the war.

5

'Baby' now had a name. Adam was born on September 18[th.] He weighed 8 pounds, 11 ounces and measured 20 inches long. Melanie (Momma) was just fine and Stan received a photograph of both in a wonderful letter from home. He placed that photo inside his flight helmet so they would always be there to remind him of his need to return to them safely.

His R&R was scheduled during the first week of November and that should mark the end of the current monsoon season. He had just been promoted to captain and was happy to give Melanie that information in his last letter. With his promotion, the allotment payments to their joint account in Abilene would automatically increase and it was just in time for the birth of Adam.

For the next five weeks or so, he would fly reconnaissance missions, weather permitting. It was apparent that 'Charlie' had been very busy during the rainy season and that his numbers of personnel and equipment in the south had increased dramatically.

Rocket attacks on the base had become more frequent and base alert status had been upgraded. A C-130 cargo aircraft, burnt to a shell as a result of one of those attacks, sat on a ramp in close proximity to the runways for all personnel to see, and another aviation fuel storage facility was burning seemingly without end.

The coming dry season would likely bring about more enemy contact for the U.S., South Vietnamese, and allied troops.

During a fairly good weather day, Captain Marks was patrolling an area north of Da Nang when informed of troops in contact, not far from his position, needing air support. As he approached the area, he was in communication with a ground commander stating that his position was taking heavy fire from enemy forces located just north and east of his location.

The captain notified tactical air command of the situation and they began looking for available strike aircraft. He then located the friendly force position and verified the location of opposing forces as indicated by the ground officer. TACP (Tactical Air Control Party) notified him that two A-1E Skyraiders were inbound with limited armament on board and they were searching for other available equipment. He then coordinated with the ground commander telling him that he was going to smoke the area as a target for strike aircraft and to let him know the accuracy of his marking.

Stan came in low and slow as he approached the area and started taking ground fire. He kept on his predetermined course and launched two 'Willie Petes.' The smoke billowed as expected and the officer in charge on the ground told him the target was just slightly west of the location marked, which was somewhat closer to the position of the friendly forces.

The lead A-1 pilot contacted Captain Marks and was informed regarding the situation. The attacking pilots saw the smoke, and Stan informed them regarding the locations of opposing forces and where they needed to strafe. The A-1 pilots went down and made the one pass they were able to, since their ammo had been depleted, and advised they were returning to their base.

The ground commander transmitted that the strafing run was of some help but he needed further assistance. Captain Marks then notified TACP; they informed him that an F-4 was close by and gave him their UHF frequency for communication. The F-4 pilot told him that he had napalm on board and that he saw the target area. The captain warned the ground officer of the impending napalm strike and gave the F-4 pilot the green light to proceed.

The result was once again devastating and Stan became concerned about the impact of that strike on friendly forces. Further contact with the ground officer indicated that things were a bit warm down there but that he was grateful for the assistance. The F-4 left the scene and Stan returned to base.

On the way back, he thought, *Why don't the damn 'Dinks'* (North Vietnamese Troops) *just pack it in and go home. How could anyone survive what we are throwing their way?* But then it dawned on him once again. Geez…they are Vietnamese and I am a visitor in Vietnam…I'm a visitor…apparently an unwelcome American visitor…and I just dumped in their backyard.

Then, while admiring and thinking of the resiliency of the Vietnamese people, Stan said to himself, "Someday on that ranch of ours back in Texas, I'm gonna have a nice hunting dog and you know what? I'm gonna name it 'Charlie.'"

It was now October. It was nearing the end of the rainy season and this marked the mid-point in Captain Marks' tour. He had been in-country for six months and was issued a second pair of jungle combat boots. This was another of those many occasions calling for celebration. And of course, he and his friends did celebrate. Airmen seemed to enjoy these releases from reality; they loved a good party. The only faces of disapproval he could detect during such celebratory performances were those of somber, oriental service workers employed at the officers' club. They seemed to be offended by the inexplicable behavior of their liberators.

This was another of those special occasions manufactured in the minds of the participants to blow off more steam. And more steam was blown off in that club in a day than by the Baltimore-Ohio Railroad during its heyday.

6

Melanie could not be more excited as she looked forward to her trip to Hawaii. Not only had she never been there before, but it was a place she always dreamed of visiting. Although busy with a newborn, she counted the days until she could see and touch her husband again. While waiting, she collected and studied travel brochures, with the intention of seeing as much as she could during this trip of a lifetime. The baby would be well taken care of by his doting grandparents, who were thrilled for Melanie and for themselves. They felt like young parents again and could not love the child more.

The young married couple was about to be reunited following a long separation that had commenced shortly after their wedding date. In the last letter Melanie received from Stan, he had asked her to book the hotel and make her travel arrangements, since he was in no position to do so. She made the hotel reservations and sent that information to her husband.

On the day of her departure, before leaving for the airport, Mr. Blake presented her with a gift-wrapped bottle of champagne to open with Stan. He was so happy for his daughter, who was ecstatic about this long-awaited reunion. The young married couple had now been separated for about seven months. In another five months or so, the family pilot should finally be flying home.

As Mr. Blake said goodbye to Melanie before she boarded her flight to Los Angeles, he reminded her to send Stan their love and let him know how much he was missed. Melanie boarded her flight with heady expectations regarding her 'honeymoon.'

Settling into her seat on the plane, she thought about Stan and all the news she wanted to share with him. Just before leaving, she decided to pack a photo album to keep her husband up-to-date with events at home. There were pictures of the baby, her mom and dad holding Adam, the nursery, his Firebird which her dad had cleaned, polished, and waxed, and pictures of the family home. She also had a surprise for him. Melanie had been saving all of the money that had been deposited in their joint bank account. Her parents would not let her spend any of their money and insisted on paying all expenses, including her plane trip to and from Hawaii, along with some spending money. They felt it was the least they could do since their son-in-law was placing his life on the line for the good of his country (as they put it). Melanie had a little savings of her own which she added to the account and it was amounting to a nice tidy sum. She believed it was an amount that would be large enough by the time he came home to start building a nice home on their land in Texas. And, she brought pictures of houses she liked for his inspection and approval.

Meanwhile, at Da Nang, Captain Marks said goodbye to his buddies, Rich and Don, after they drove him to the aerial port on base to board his flight to Hawaii. The U.S Government had contracted with civilian air carriers to transport troops to and from R&R locations. His friends left him at the aerial port well ahead of his scheduled departure time and he awaited further instructions.

While waiting, he thought about stories other soldiers had shared with him regarding their R&R exploits. Rich was a single man; he had already taken his R&R trip to Sydney, Australia. Stan and Don had spent hours with him, over drinks, looking at photographs and listening to joyous tales regarding his escapades. Rich met a young, lovely, Aussie 'bird' who had immigrated to Australia from England with her parents as a young girl. His descriptions of her did not do her justice. She appeared even more attractive in his photos, and Rich was now corresponding with her on a regular basis. Talk about long distance relationships. Wow, he wished Rich luck with this one.

Lieutenant Marks was dressed in his Class A uniform, as required for the flight, which made passengers easily recognizable throughout the waiting area. It was obvious to all that they were the latest group of lucky soldiers granted a much-needed respite from rigors endured for months. Every seat on the flight would be taken since there was plenty of competition for available spaces. The passengers waited for a couple of hours and the scheduled boarding time went by. Rumors were starting to circulate about mechanical problems with the aircraft that would be taking them to Hawaii.

Finally, an announcement was made stating that, in fact, there was a mechanical problem with the aircraft and a new boarding time was announced for two hours later. This was not good news, but these were soldiers serving in a war zone. They were not used to receiving 'good news.' This was just par for the course. Two hours later, there was still no boarding announcement and they continued to wait. Finally, an announcement was made stating that another two hours was needed to prepare the aircraft. Of course, as a pilot, Captain Marks knew the importance of maintenance functions, but

Melanie would be waiting for him in Hawaii and he had no way of contacting her regarding the reason for delay.

The additional waiting time also passed and an announcement was then made stating that the aircraft would not be ready until the following morning. This was hard to take and groans among the passengers were clearly audible. After serving many months in country, they were all losing one day of their precious seven day R&R.

They collectively thought, *Okay, now what?* And then were herded together and marched off to a large open barracks area – open meaning that doors and windows had not been installed in frames on the two-story wood building. Rows of bunk beds were lined up inside, and each one of the soldiers grabbed a bunk and stowed the little gear he had. The mattresses were bare, but the weather was hot and humid; there was no need for anything more.

It appeared that few, if any, passengers knew each other and that they had all come from separate units. The one thing they had in common was that they were all tired. Many of these soldiers appeared quite comfortable as they collapsed on mattresses and fell fast asleep. It was probable that some had come from the bush and had not enjoyed such luxury in quite a while. But that was not the case with Captain Marks. He had become accustomed to air-conditioned comfort, and another potential problem was the swarms of mosquitoes. However, the passengers were all very tired and as a result, the mosquitoes had little to no effect on anyone, including Stan. The insects enjoyed a feast and their hosts got some much-needed rest. Thank goodness for all those quinine tablets Captain Marks had religiously taken to ward off malaria. Within a short period, the soldiers were asleep and all was quiet. Experienced soldiers get all the sleep they can whenever they can and wherever they can.

Meanwhile, it had been a long trip from Abilene, Texas to Honolulu, Hawaii. Melanie was exhausted, but marveled at the beauty of the island of Oahu as the airplane approached the Honolulu Airport. The taxi ride to the hotel was a pleasure. Palm trees swaying in the breeze with beautiful beaches beyond was a sight to behold. She checked into a high-rise hotel, where a porter took her luggage and escorted her to her accommodations. The suite was spacious and elegant, offering a spectacular view of Diamond Head. This was indeed the honeymoon she had always dreamed of and was expecting her husband to arrive any minute.

Melanie unpacked her bags and freshened up for her reunion with the man she loved. Waiting for him to arrive, she browsed through some brochures placed on a desk. When an hour had gone by, she started to wonder about Stan. She decided to call the airport and check on the status of his flight. The agent informed her that the flight had been delayed and was rescheduled to arrive the following afternoon.

Hearing this news, she sat on the edge of the bed and cried. She was so disappointed. How could this be happening? She had waited so long for this time together and now they were going to lose a whole day and she would have to spend the entire time alone. How awful.

After a few minutes, Melanie composed herself and walked over to the window, where she regarded the amazing view. Oh, how she wanted to share this moment with Stan. A small balcony with a table and two chairs was just beyond the sliding glass doors. Melanie opened the door and stepped out onto the balcony. A pleasant breeze lifted her spirits somewhat and she decided to order a room service meal for herself rather than dine alone in the hotel restaurant.

Waiting for the meal to be delivered, Melanie thought about her husband and how disappointed he must be after all he had been through recently. She began to feel a little guilty about feeling sorry for herself and owed it to Stan to keep her chin up. After all, she was enjoying luxurious accommodations and God knows what he was dealing with.

Dinner arrived and Melanie spent time on the balcony taking in the wonders of her new surroundings. She thought about how much she loved and missed her overdue husband and decided to plan their sightseeing itinerary for when he finally did arrive. There was so much she wanted to do and so much she wanted to see, but did not really want to do any of it without her man. *Come on Stan,* she thought, *please hurry, I've waited so long and I miss you so much.* But then she realized, *If I made it this far, I can certainly get through just one more day. Can't I?*

Exhaustion finally got the better of Melanie and she slept through the night dreaming of Stan and Adam and the house they would build back home in Texas.

At Da Nang, Captain Marks and his fellow passengers awoke looking sweaty and disheveled. Few words were exchanged as they awaited information regarding the status of their flight. Suddenly, intermittent squeals could be detected from a public address system along with sounds of someone attempting to clear his throat. The announcer reported that the aircraft had been repaired during the evening hours and was ready for boarding. The half-awake crowd of soldiers suddenly came to life and cheers filled the air.

The motley crew boarded the aircraft in need of showers, shaves, and clean clothes. Most of them were young married men about to meet wives that they had not seen in months, and this was probably not the way they had foreseen that encounter. None of them had much luggage to stow on the aircraft since they were all used to living a spartan existence. Captain Marks checked to ensure he still had the present he had purchased for Melanie a month or so prior to his departure. He had ordered a white gold, heart-shaped necklace embedded with tiny blue sapphires from a PACEX (Pacific Exchange) catalog provided to soldiers serving in Southeast Asia. It was there and when he was satisfied that his carry-on bag was safely stowed away, he took his seat.

As the aircraft lifted from the runway surface, another loud cheer arose from the passenger cabin. For many of them, this was the first time their bodies had been separated from the soil they had come to loathe. These soldiers had just spent months risking their lives attempting to liberate a foreign land from its own countrymen. If that was not confusing enough, they had also been attempting to protect the folks back home from…what the hell was it they were protecting them from? Well, anyway, they had a temporary reprieve from that mind-numbing exercise in patriotism. The captain looked around, smiled, and thought, *Enjoy yourselves now guys and I sure hope that we all make it to that 'Freedom Bird' flight we are all yearning to board sometime down the road.*

It was a long flight to Honolulu and yes, most of them were fast asleep in no time.

Melanie woke up late that morning and when she realized just how late it was, she was grateful, not only for a restful sleep, but for the time that had passed, thereby reducing her wait for Stan. She showered, dressed, and ordered room service once again for breakfast. While waiting for the meal to arrive, she called the airport to check on the status of his flight.

176

She was told that the flight was inbound to Honolulu and was scheduled to arrive in about three and one half hours.

While eating her breakfast, she decided to take a cab to the airport and await his arrival. That beat sitting around the hotel room and it might be a welcome surprise for him, since the original plan called for him to meet her at the hotel.

Prior to taking the cab, she stopped by the front desk and asked the clerk to inform her husband, Captain Marks, that she had gone to the airport to meet him in the event that they missed each other.

"Captain Marks?" the clerk asked.

"Yes, he's an Air Force captain on R&R from Vietnam and he's meeting me here," Melanie replied.

The clerk smiled. "Oh yes, of course, I certainly will."

Four

Cease Fire

1

The approach to Honolulu Airport was even more beautiful than Stan remembered the same experience seven long months ago. Of course, at that time, he was heading away from home and all that he truly loved. This time, he was heading toward home and perhaps his long-awaited reunion with Melanie had something to do with his perceptions of increased beauty. *Damn right it did,* he thought. He smiled broadly, his heart leapt, and his mind was a euphoric whirlwind as his aircraft finally touched down on the runway.

Once again a loud, joyous, roar went up from the war-weary occupants enclosed in a civilian commercial aircraft. Only America could make this happen…only America did make this happen. They were alive and well and were being reunited with loved ones. Don't think about next week; don't spoil this; be happy. Forget the past and do not think about the future. "Let's make the best of this little bit of heaven" seemed about the best way to appraise the occasion.

As the aircraft taxied clear of the runway, he recalled something Rich had told him about his R&R to Sydney, Australia, and wondered if he was about to experience another delay. After Rich's flight landed in Sydney, it was parked on a ramp area some distance from the passenger terminal. A mobile staircase was brought to the front entrance and put in place. Rich thought that strange and the passengers all waited for an explanation. About fifteen minutes later, an airport vehicle drove up to the aircraft and two men exited carrying some kind of small equipment as they proceeded toward the aircraft. They entered the plane wearing masks. The two men were holding spray cans and they proceeded down the aisle toward the rear of the aircraft. One man began spraying the left side and the other the right side as they proceeded toward the front of the cabin. When that operation was complete, they left the plane, entered their vehicle, and drove off.

The young men aboard Rich's aircraft were used to taking orders and handling whatever came their way. This was just another of those occurrences. Sheep do not require explanations as they are herded off to be shorn or to be slaughtered for that matter. Were they being deloused prior to allowing them to mingle with the local population? It appeared that way. Rich thought there must have been some reason for that treatment; he figured it was a good one, but wondered what it was.

Stan was now wondering if that would happen to his flight and was relieved when his aircraft taxied to the passenger terminal without further delay. The men waited for permission to deplane and began to retrieve their gear. Stan was somewhere near the middle of the cabin and, as a result, quite a few men were ahead of him as they meandered slowly toward the front of the plane. These soldiers were about to re-enter 'the world' they had left behind and their first view of it was just awesome. The waiting area was full of beautiful, young American women. They were the wives and girlfriends of soldiers exiting the plane. Here they were back in the arms of the women they longed for. What could be better than this?

Stan enjoyed the spectacle, but did not expect to see Melanie in the crowd. He planned to find a taxi cab to take him to the hotel. Meanwhile, Melanie was anxiously surveying the large number of military personnel wearing uniforms of different service branches and strained to find an Air Force captain. The men did not look much like the servicemen she was accustomed to seeing stateside. They were not clean-shaven, their uniforms were soiled and unkempt. She then saw a tall Air Force captain in the middle of the pack moving at a pace somewhat faster than the others, and he was headed away from the crowd. Melanie was not sure if it was her husband. This man was darker and thinner than the Stan she remembered and he had a mustache. But, as she looked again, she realized that it must be him because no one else walked like that; it had to be him.

She ran toward him and shouted, "Stan, I'm over here." He kept walking, at a fast pace, which she had difficulty keeping up with. In fear of losing sight of him, she yelled at the top of her lungs, "Stan, turn around I'm over here. I'm over here Stan."

He stopped in his tracks, turned around, and looked back at the crowd. With a puzzled expression on his face, he saw a beautiful young woman racing toward him. She had shoulder-length, dark hair, longer than he recalled since her WAF days, and was wearing a short white dress. When he realized it was Melanie, he raced toward her as well. As they embraced and kissed each other, the crowd went wild, cheering and smiling at a spectacle usually reserved for the silver screen. The reunited couple barely heard the applause; they just looked at each other with tears in their eyes as they proclaimed their love for each other. The occasion begged for a photograph; this was the picture of happiness.

During the cab ride to their hotel, Mr. and Mrs. Marks could not keep their hands off of each other. At one point, Melanie whispered, "Stan, what's with this mustache? Don't think I can get used to that."

He answered, "Oh, just something guys do over there, I guess. Don't worry though, when we get to the hotel, it comes off right away." She smiled with appreciation. During brief interludes between hugging and kissing, they marveled at the beauty of the scenery, and Melanie showed her husband recent photographs of Adam. He was overwhelmed with love for this little person who looked so much like him, with wide-set blue eyes and light blond hair.

Stan caught an occasional glimpse of the cab driver's smiling face through the rear-view mirror, but that did not hamper their activity in the least. The driver pulled up to the entrance of the hotel. Stan exited, walked to the opposite side of the car like the gentleman he was, and opened the door for 'Lady Melanie.' He then walked back to the other side toward the cabby standing near the driver-side door and said, "How much do I owe you, sir?"

The driver looked at him and asked, "R&R from Vietnam, Captain?"

With a smile, he replied, "That's right. It's been seven long months and I'm happy as hell."

"Bet you are and I'll bet your lady is as well," declared the driver. He re-entered the cab and said, "This is on me. Enjoy your stay in Hawaii, Captain." And he drove away.

Stan loved the hotel and complimented Melanie's choice of accommodations. She excitedly stated, "Wait till you see the view from our room and the balcony is just special."

Melanie waved to the desk clerk as they walked past. Smiling, she pointed to her husband. He returned the smile and waved as well.

As the couple entered their room, he looked around with approval and remarked, "Beautiful, just beautiful and you are so right, just look at that view! Is that Diamond Head over there?"

"Yes, it is, and what is this over here?" she asked, referring to a fresh fruit basket and bottle of champagne which had been placed on a small table nearby.

She opened the envelope attached and the note inside read, 'Compliments of the hotel. Enjoy your R&R.' Melanie smiled and handed the note to Stan. As he read it, she pulled out another bottle of champagne given to them by her father. They laughed and embraced while thinking of the wonderful honeymoon they were about to enjoy.

"Please Stan," she said suddenly. "Please shave that mustache and please take a shower."

"I'll do that right now," he responded, "but first, I have something for you."

He presented Melanie with the stone-encrusted, heart-shaped, necklace that he had so carefully chosen. She was surprised that he had been able to acquire such an item during his tour and was delighted to receive it.

While he showered and shaved, she donned an alluring negligee purchased for this special occasion. After pouring two glasses of champagne, she placed a 'do not disturb' sign on the door, locked it, sat down, and waited for her man. The rest of the evening was a very special and private affair not available for public consumption. You will all just have to rely upon your imaginations and let's hope they are extremely vivid indeed.

A more wonderful honeymoon is hard to imagine...the sweetness of reunion after such a long, heart-breaking separation, the birth of a child, and news, so much news to share.

Melanie informed Stan that she would be teaching English at her old high school in Abilene – the same school where her parents had taught and where they were once students. She would start at the beginning of the next semester after the New Year holiday, and her parents would care for the baby, Adam, while she was at work.

He was happy for her after hearing that this was something she really wanted to do. He then revealed his intention to leave the Air Force when his service commitment was fulfilled and was considering other options. Melanie could not be more delighted and relieved because it was so difficult to endure such painful separations. Also, for the sake of their children, she believed it would be best if he was at home and became a vital part of their development.

Melanie asked him what he had in mind after leaving the service and he reminded her that he still had about a year and a half left on his service commitment after returning from Vietnam. His goal was to secure a T-37 instructor pilot slot at Laughlin Air Force Base during that period, if possible.

"That would be great. You could drive to Abilene during breaks, hopefully on weekends, when I'm not working," she said, "and after?"

"Well, after that, I suppose a civilian flying job or air traffic control with the Federal Aviation Administration (FAA) makes sense."

Melanie looked at him thoughtfully and asked, "Stan, have you ever thought about teaching?"

He replied, "No, not really. What are you thinking?"

"I'm thinking that you are a college graduate with technical experience, and that is hard to find in our school district. There are always openings for teachers with that type of background at the high school where I'll be teaching. I was lucky to get an English teacher slot; those jobs are not as difficult to fill.

He was listening attentively. "Hmm, really think that's possible?"

She was enthusiastic about the prospect. "I know it's possible. Are you kidding, we are practically begging for candidates with your background to pursue teaching careers. Seriously, if you don't get the job, no one will. Interested?"

Stan was definitely interested. "You bet I am. Thanks for that. I need a change and this sounds great. We would be together and with the time off such a career offers, we would be able to make up for a lot of lost time."

"Alright. Now that that is settled, take a look at this and tell me what you think?" With that, she pulled a folder from a drawer and showed him a variety of plans for a house to be built on their property.

He was impressed. "Wow, these are nice, but can we afford to do this?"

Without a word, Melanie showed him the balance in their joint account. The look on her husband's face was incredulous. "Good Lord, where did all that come from?" he asked.

She explained how she had been able to save with the help of her parents, and that with his promotion and her new job, they could easily afford to go ahead. She further explained the low building costs in their area and that her parents were giving them an interest-free loan to complete the project payable only when they felt comfortable doing so. "What do you think?" she asked.

"Think? I think it's fantastic. Please thank your parents for me. I can't tell you how much I appreciate all of their support."

"I think they already know that and that's partially why they are so happy to be of help. But yes, I will certainly let them know."

The weather had been beautiful during their time together and they toured such places as the World War II Pearl Harbor monuments and enjoyed the sun, sand, and surf. It was indeed a glorious honeymoon, but once again, they needed to prepare for another painful separation. During dinner the last evening before Melanie needed to catch her flight, they promised that they would be strong for each other and for the sake of little Adam.

They held hands during the entire cab ride to the airport and looked at each other almost constantly. They were no longer interested in the scenery; they were now only interested in each other. With love in their eyes and pain in their hearts, they were forced to travel great distances apart. Their lives together had just begun and the question on their minds was one that would never reach their lips. Would they ever see each other again?

2

Melanie returned to the ranch and eagerly planned a new home for her small family. Baby Adam was doing just fine and Mr. and Mrs. Blake had been happy to hear all about their daughter's wonderful Hawaii honeymoon.

Stan flew back to Da Nang enthusiastic about future prospects and determined to finish his current tour. When he entered his hooch, it became apparent that he had a new roommate, considering the gear in the room belonging to another airman. He walked back down the hallway and knocked on Rich's door. Don told him to come in. After exchanging informal greetings and small talk about R&R in Hawaii, he asked Don if he had met his new roommate. Don did meet him briefly. His name was Jack, a first lieutenant O-2 pilot; he seemed like a nice guy just feeling his way around, and he was looking forward to meeting Stan.

With that, he returned to his room and began catching up on correspondence. After being away for a week, he had letters sitting on his desk from friends and family that needed to be read and answered. As Stan was attending to his writing, Jack appeared at the door and introduced himself. He had already met other members of the unit while Stan was away and indicated that he had recently been given the usual grand tours and briefings provided by Major Bannon.

Jack had just returned from his day at operations and the new roommates were both hungry. They walked over to the officers' club at the other side of the main compound and exchanged information regarding their background. Jack was a single, good-looking, young man without a steady girlfriend. He was from Kentucky, drank bourbon, and graduated from the University of Kentucky with a degree in political science. Jack reminded him a little of Eric in that he appeared to be carefree, adventurous, and on the prowl for skirts. Stan told him that he had five months left in country and that he would be glad to answer any questions he might have regarding operations.

It suddenly dawned on Stan that Major Bannon, Tom, Dick, and Harry must be about ready to rotate back to 'the world.' They had been in country before he arrived and could not have much time left. He asked Jack if there had been any excitement during his absence and Jack responded that everything he sees on the flight line is exciting. Just about any kind of aircraft in the inventory of every branch of the service seemed to be operating there, and all under combat conditions. Stan laughed and said that the base is a joy for military science students. "You want to learn and know about it, you'll probably find it here."

Captain Marks decided that he did not want to partake in any late night partying and that he would try to set an example for the newly arrived lieutenant by getting a good night's rest in preparation for a day at the office tomorrow. They finished their dinner, had a drink, returned to the hooch, and had a 'rack attack' (went to sleep).

Next morning, during breakfast, the guys kidded Stan about the absence of his mustache. "Melanie didn't like the hair lip, huh?"

He laughed. "No, and I wasn't about to waste any time trying to change her mind. After all, we did lose one day of R&R as it was."

And he explained the situation regarding the aircraft mechanical problem as they all groaned in sympathy for the young married couple.

Then Stan questioned them about their DEROS (Date of Estimated Return from Overseas). They happily responded that they would all be gone within the next month and that their replacements should be arriving shortly.

"Major Bannon, do you know who your replacement will be yet?" he asked.

"Yes, I do. He's a lieutenant colonel by the name of Frank Simmons. This will be his second tour. He served as an FAC during his last tour when he was promoted from captain to major."

"Do you know him well?" He asked with surprise and interest. It seemed a little odd to him that promotions could be achieved so quickly.

Everyone looked at each other and Major Bannon cleared his throat. "I know of him, Stan. That is, I know his reputation."

Captain Marks surveyed the expressions on everyone's faces and decided that he needed more information.

"And?" he prodded.

Major Bannon continued, "And he earned that promotion, Stan. He was very daring. He did things that I taught you guys not to do and he was lucky enough to survive. Be careful, I hear that he's not a guy to be fooled with."

Words to the wise, he thought and decided to change the subject since the mood was becoming a little tense.

"Hey, I have an idea; as if you haven't thought about it already. Let's have one big celebration for all you guys since you're leaving about the same time. Bet we can put that fighter pilot squadron to shame. What do you say?"

"Hell yeah we can. Let's do it" was the unanimous response.

Jack, as the new guy, just observed and listened to what was going on, deciding that he would talk things over with Stan later. But his facial expressions and body language indicated that his main interest was in a blowout, wild, going away party.

The guys all flew a few more rather uneventful missions and Jack got his feet wet. A program called 'Vietnamization' had been going on now for some time and things were slowly changing in country as a result. The 'powers that be' had decided to transfer many functions performed by American troops over to the Vietnamese as American troop strength in country was being gradually decreased. Rich had been telling Stan about the VNAF personnel his unit has been training at the RAPCON to eventually take over those duties. The newer gear arriving at the base was being turned over to the Vietnamese for their use while Americans continued to use the older equipment.

During the party, Stan just let it all hang out. He had grown close to these guys and they had taught him a lot. He may even owe them his life as a result of those lessons. As the party developed and as others from additional outfits became aware of the reason for the ballyhoo, the celebration eventually took over most of the club. And yes, the fighter pilots became a big part of the celebration.

It was also brought to Stan's attention, by the major, that Jack had a new friend. Jack was over in a corner with a pretty, young Vietnamese girl and they seemed to be involved in activity other than just linguistics training. He took note of this and decided to have a later conversation with Jack.

I Corps was Marine country. Da Nang was in the I Corps area and the base had been protected chiefly through the efforts of American Marines as well as Army, Air Force, ARVN, VNAF personnel, and others. But the Marines were being withdrawn gradually as South Vietnamese forces were trained to absorb their duties along with the others mentioned. The North Vietnamese had been taking advantage of poor weather conditions for months now, and apparently supplies had been flowing south along the Ho Chi Minh Trail in support of their numbers in the south. It was believed that much of the equipment and personnel transported were coming in from Laos, on the western border of Vietnam.

Stan thought a lot about what he was observing and tried to put it all into perspective. He was trying to make sense of all this. America had been engaged in this action for years now and it was tearing his country apart. Anti-war protests back home were increasing in size and their influence was growing. A number of prime time television shows were devoted to the growing anti-war sentiment and many of the newly arriving draftees in Vietnam, having been exposed to all of this, were describing the action back home to those already serving in country. Many young Americans had fled the United States to avoid the draft and were residing in such places as Canada and Sweden.

He thought about the history of his country and found so many similarities between the current situation and those existing in the colonies during the American Revolution. About half of the colonists remained loyal to the King of England and the others, called patriots by us today and rebels by the English back then, wanted to be free of domination from an overseas power. Vietnam was now a country divided between a communist regime in the north and a not so trustworthy, so-called, democracy in the south. Like the patriots of old, the South Vietnamese needed to be wary of infiltrators and those providing intelligence to the opposition.

He recalled that the American colonies had been dominated by a powerful European nation interested in exploiting resources much as France and Japan had been in Vietnam. It appeared to him that his country had recently fallen prey to its own idealism and believing it necessary to save the world from the scourge of communism embarked on a crusade to end its expansion here and now.

What about the Vietnamese? This is their country. What is it that they want? Why should they not want what everyone else wants? Why not leave them alone to decide their own destiny?

Stan recalled that one of his boyhood heroes, President John F. Kennedy, indicated shortly before his death that the Vietnamese question needed to be resolved by the Vietnamese people. And he could not help but wonder if he would have ever found himself in this country had JFK lived.

3

The old warriors departed the scene and their replacements arrived. Colonel Simmons wasted no time making his presence known. Except for him, Stan was now the old man in their small group. The words of Major Bannon were not forgotten and Stan kept a close eye on his new commander.

Alert status at the base was at a high level, due to intelligence reports regarding enemy ground activity, and nighttime rocket attacks had increased in their frequency, tending to confirm that reports of supplies flowing to the south along the Ho Chi Minh Trail were not unfounded.

The colonel joined his new charges and flew what he considered training missions. He identified terrain needing detailed reconnaissance as he explained operations conducted during his previous tour. During one of those training missions, they received a report of troops in contact and the colonel led his flight to the location indicated. As they approached the site, they tuned in the FM frequency assigned and Colonel Simmons contacted the ground commander. The Army officer on the ground gave detailed information regarding the size and location of the enemy force that appeared to far outnumber his own. The colonel contacted the tactical air control party and informed them of assistance required.

The position of the enemy force needed to be marked for identification and the colonel told Captain Marks that when he gave the word, he wanted him to show the new guys how it was done. TACP notified the colonel that two A-1s were on their way and then instructed him to mark the target zone.

Stan contacted the ground commander to verify that the situation had not changed and transmitted that he wanted to pinpoint the area for attack aircraft. He was given the go ahead and descended his plane toward the location described. As he approached that area, he started taking ground fire but continued inbound at low altitude. His aircraft was hit several times before he launched white phosphorous rockets at the designated target zone. He then climbed, turned toward the rest of his flight, and observed the white plumes of smoke emerge from the forestation below. The ground commander indicated that the marking was slightly east of the exact location needed and Stan replied that the fighter aircraft, inbound to the target area, would be notified of that discrepancy.

He then turned his attention to the condition of his aircraft by checking his instruments and informing the colonel that he had taken hits. He flew his aircraft within view of the other pilots and asked for visual checks. They reported nothing unusual.

The A-1 flight leader checked in reporting that the target area was in sight. Stan notified him that he needed to attack just west of the target as indicated and was 'rogered' by the A-1 pilot. He then rechecked with the ground commander to ensure that nothing had changed. The ground officer in charge replied that he was taking casualties and needed medevac (medical evacuation) support. Stan 'rogered' that communication, gave a green light to the A-1 flight leader to proceed with the attack, and then notified TACP of the need for medevac equipment.

The A-1 Skyraiders went in low and reported taking ground fire as they strafed the area as instructed. As they climbed away from the target, Stan checked in with the ground commander who indicated that he needed equipment for the evacuation of at least six of his personnel and that there would probably be more by the time they arrived. He also stated that he needed additional fighter support closer to his location than the previous strike.

The A-1s were sent back in for a second run and were given instructions regarding changes indicated by the officer on the ground. Stan then notified TACP regarding the additional casualties. After the second strafing run, the ground commander indicated that they now had the situation under control, but he needed that medevac quickly. Stan told him that choppers were on the way.

With that, the ground commander thanked him for the assist and said, "Hey, I know you, don't I? Aren't you Stan Marks?"

"Hell yes," he replied. "No, don't tell me now…is this Bart Small?"

"Goddam straight it is, boy. You take care now you hear, and you keep in touch. When we get state side, I'm gonna buy you one hell of a drink and don't be surprised if I give you one great big kiss."

"Thanks, but let's just make it a hug, okay? Hey, your choppers are here. Is the LZ (Landing Zone) hot (under fire)?"

"No, they're okay. Bring 'em in."

"Okay dude. You take care now. See ya."

The colonel then cut in telling the flight to return to base for debriefing.

On the unit's ramp area at Da Nang, Stan looked over the condition of his plane and observed a number of holes, but did not see anything that appeared to be of major concern. One of the maintenance personnel, an airman known to Stan as Louie, saw him looking over the plane and said, "Damn sir, looks like you've had a fun day, huh?"

"We all get lucky sometimes Louie and this was Charlie's lucky day. I don't ever intend to let him get this lucky again. Will you please check things out for me and make sure my ship is okay?"

"Will do, sir, no problem."

The rest of the pilots in the flight gathered around and began to inspect the condition of his plane. The colonel approached them and said, "Okay guys, inside NOW."

They stowed their gear and assembled in the briefing room. Colonel Simmons complimented Captain Marks on his job performance and said, "How the hell did you know that guy?"

"Oh, we were in college together, sir."

"College? American colleges are a hotbed of liberal, hippy-type freaks, and commie, pinko, rats. Where the hell did you go to college?"

"Don't recall seeing any of those at The Citadel, sir."

"Okay, that explains it," he countered, cracking a rare smile, "I guess you wouldn't have seen any of those and by the way, nice job. Anyone have any questions for Captain Marks?"

There were none, and the colonel instructed him to show the new guys how to file the after action report.

That night, Stan had a little talk with Jack about his new Vietnamese friend.

"Jack, that little Vietnamese honey I saw you with sure is cute. What's her name?"

"Not really sure, but it sounds something like Tai Wan. I just call her Tai. I'm not really interested in her conversation though if you get my drift. I taught her how to say something that sounds like Jack, and she says that 'I number one GI,'" he said with a laugh.

"Jack, you know, around here we don't know who we can trust and who we can't trust. You'll need to be careful what you say around her. A lot of folks are depending on us to keep activity under our hats. Those 'grunts' (infantry soldiers) out there don't need us spilling beans about our operations."

"Aw, don't worry, Stan. She hardly understands a word I say."

"Let's hope not, Jack. But just the same, keep your talk restricted to other than our work. Okay?"

"Gotcha Stan. No problem."

During a few more training sessions with the colonel, he began to see what Major Bannon meant about the colonel taking risks. The colonel would fly low and slow, and then return almost immediately to recheck the area once again in an attempt to draw ground fire. So far, nothing happened.

After a few of these attempts at suicide, the colonel briefed his unit on what he expected of them. He advised them that they needed to draw ground fire if they ever expected to reduce the amount of enemy activity in the area. He told them that he had reviewed the reports filed within the unit during the past year and was disappointed in the number of contacts made with the enemy. That needed to change, he said, and he wanted the unit's tactics to improve. The colonel then addressed Stan. "Captain Marks, why do you think this unit's contact with Charlie has been so limited?"

He answered, "Well sir, when I first arrived, it was at the end of a dry season and then with the onset of a rainy season, our operations were hindered significantly. Of course, the weather has now changed and I expect the frequency of our contact will change as well."

The colonel nodded and continued questioning Stan.

"Captain, when you descend on a suspected area of activity, do you ever return to recheck that area?"

"Yes sir. Quite often actually. Usually do that on the return trip."

"Return trip? Why don't you do it right away?"

"So as not to become a target, sir. The first pass alerts them and, if they are there, they'll be waiting for me on the second pass."

"Exactly, Captain, and that is what I want you to do. Our job is to make them shoot at us so that we can get them. Got it, Captain? You saw me do that numerous times now. Have you not, Captain?"

"Yes sir, I have. But I have never seen them fire upon your aircraft during such maneuvers. We need you to show us how to avoid being shot down. The men in this unit want very much to do their jobs sir, but it doesn't seem wise to take such unnecessary risks. That is not the way we have been trained to conduct our missions."

The colonel was visibly angry. His face was turning a fiery red, his eyes bulged, and Stan could swear that smoke was emanating from his nostrils.

"Are you refusing to obey my orders, Captain?"

"No sir, I am not. I will gladly follow your orders once you have trained me properly so that I may follow your instructions."

"That will be all," barked the colonel and he dismissed his pilots.

Outside the building and out of earshot of the colonel, the other guys gathered around Stan and told him to be careful because it appears the old man is hot on his tail.

"Yeah, I know. Thanks guys."

They flew more training missions with the colonel and he failed at every attempt to draw fire. After returning to base one day, the colonel called him aside and said he wanted to talk to him in private. He thought, *Oh damn, what in hell is he up to now?*

Colonel Simmons briefed him about an upcoming operation designated as Lam Son 719. Because intelligence gathering indicated that increased supplies to enemy forces were entering from Laos, incursions would be made into that country to stem the flow. However, U.S. forces were not permitted by the American government to enter that country on the ground. The plan called for ARVN troops to conduct ground operations supported by American artillery and air power based in South Vietnam. As a result, the U.S. Army was reopening the base at Khe Sahn to support the mission. That base was located about ten miles east of the Laotian border. The Army was in need of radio equipment for its air traffic control operations at Khe Sahn and the colonel wanted Captain Marks to fly it in.

Stan was well aware of the reputation of Khe Sahn. A bitter battle had been waged there in 1968 with heavy losses taken by both sides and had supposedly been the bloodiest battle of the war. The base had been abandoned by the Army at that time and was now being reopened. The runway that he needed to land his aircraft on was a temporarily installed metal strip runway a little more than 3,000 feet long as opposed to the approximate 10,000 feet of runway at Da Nang.

Stan was a bit wary of Colonel Simmons and somewhat apprehensive regarding this mission. The flight to Khe Sahn afforded him some time to think and his thoughts brought about more questions. *What were we trying to accomplish here and how do we intend to accomplish our goals? Damn,* he thought, *seems to me that the only mission here is to figure out how to survive this tour of duty long enough before we will be allowed to go back home.*

As he approached the base, he viewed the dirty, dusty, hole in the ground trying desperately to pass itself off as an airfield. His aircraft was not fired upon while on final approach to the runway and during his approach, he observed ground equipment and personnel busy at work apparently preparing the area for operations. He observed a couple of O-1 Army, bird dog, FAC aircraft alongside the runway and a couple of small Huey helicopters. At the end of the runway, an Air Force C-130 aircraft was being unloaded.

Captain Marks pulled off to the side of the runway near an Army, air traffic control, GCA unit and exited his plane. He unloaded the radio equipment and carried it over to the GCA trailer. A soldier, who appeared weary and detached, took the equipment from him. The man seemed to be physically located at Khe Sahn but firmly established elsewhere psychologically. No words were exchanged and Stan walked back toward his aircraft.

He then thought, *I'll probably never see this place again.* At least, he hoped that he would not, and believed he was observing an important part of what would very soon be recorded history. He also remembered that he had a Minolta 35 mm camera and film that he had purchased through a PACEX (Pacific Exchange) catalog stowed aboard his plane.

He retrieved the camera and started taking pictures of anything that caught his interest starting with the GCA unit.

It suddenly struck him as he looked around that he was in the middle of something very dangerous. This was once the scene of deadly combat and it was being rebuilt in preparation for additional action. Everything was dirty and dusty, including all of the personnel busily occupied in the area.

Stan felt a bit out of place, since he was neat and clean in his fresh fatigues, but decided that he must take photographs. This was something that should have been documented.

The control tower was striking and he took a picture of that structure. It was a mobile unit that appeared to be large enough to support only one occupant, surrounded and supported by mounds of sand bags. He observed large craters in the ground covered by some sort of tent-like canvas erections; he photographed those and walked around one of them to identify its purpose. There was an opening at the opposite side of the unique construction and as he peered within, he observed a shelter area housing a soldier with his back turned toward him. The walls of the crude dwelling were composed of what appeared to be a red clay dirt and the GI within was shaving as he peered into a small glass mirror embedded in a dirt wall. Stan felt like an intruder and walked away.

He then walked toward the C-130 aircraft, parked at the end of the runway, which had just been unloaded. The unloaded cargo appeared to be pallets of artillery shells. That made sense to him considering the briefing given to him by the colonel prior to his departure from Da Nang. Evidently, those shells were to be used in support of the South Vietnamese incursion into Laos for the Lam Son 719 Operation. The pallets were being transported from the area and he could also see ARVN (South Vietnamese) troops in the vicinity of the C-130 transport aircraft. As he approached that plane, he realized that they were wounded South Vietnamese soldiers probably waiting to board the C-130 for medical treatment at Da Nang.

After taking all of this in, Stan thought, *Okay, enough of this stuff, this is as close to the history of this place as I wish to get. Thank God my plane is over there and, with any luck, I may live long enough to understand what the hell this is all about. Please...someone...tell me that we are good people doing what we need to do for a worthy cause. Please let me know that my friends' lives are being sacrificed for praiseworthy purpose. Please!!!*

4

Departure from Khe Sahn was fortunately a routine event, but not in Stan's mind. He was certain that what he witnessed would remain with him for the rest of his days and that was not a comforting thought. The losses incurred for purposes he did not fully understand were beyond his belief. His own sacrifices were extreme enough, he thought, but what these guys were subjected to seemed incredible, considering that most of them probably had no idea why they were even there.

On his return flight to Da Nang, he made a few low passes in areas that he thought could be hot spots, but did not detect any activity. He realized that his eyes had become much more accustomed to the terrain, and that he could now discern objects that he was unable to detect formerly. During one pass, he considered doing what the colonel wanted him to do, but remembered Major Bannon's advice regarding the colonel, and also about making second passes so soon. He decided that he preferred taking the major's advice and that the colonel was perhaps a little, as Jack's little Vietnamese Tai would say, "Dinky Dau" (crazy in the head).

He was halfway through his remaining five months in country now and was really missing his little family back in Texas. He thought about what his father-in-law told him on the trip to the airport when he left for the Philippines. It was something like, "You will get to return home someday, those poor Vietnamese are already home."

He rarely saw Jack anymore after duty hours. Jack was much too busy canoodling with the lovely Mai Tai or, so sorry, was it Tai Wan? *Ah yes, that was it. It was Tai Wan,* he thought. He hoped it wouldn't cause Jack too much trouble, but it did give him a lot of free time alone in their room at night, and he was grateful for it.

Stan wrote long heartfelt letters to Melanie asking about their baby, Adam, and how her new job as a high school teacher was going. He was also excited to hear about how the plans for their new home were progressing. When he received her return letters, he was able to transport himself mentally and emotionally thousands of miles from his present location to a simple and beautiful life with his wife and their child. How he wished he could hold his little boy in his arms, feed him, tell him how much he loved him, and just be with him. Adam would be about six months old when he returned home, and he took comfort in the fact that he would see the child often after that. As for Melanie, that was his reason for doing all that he was doing. His mission, military, or otherwise, was to survive his current ordeal and return home to her forever.

In the meantime, there was Colonel Simmons to deal with. Since returning from Khe Sahn, they had not been able to identify any enemy ground activity or draw any ground fire. Stan believed the odds were in favor of it happening sooner rather than later.

Captain Marks and one of the new young lieutenants were following the colonel in a loose formation on this beautiful day for flying, even if it was another day in Vietnam. He still admired the beauty of the country from the air as much as he despised the activity on the ground. But then there were many more people on the ground than in the air. Isn't it usually the case that where people tend to congregate you find the most trouble and conflict? Isn't it human nature and hasn't it always been human nature that has brought about controversy, animosity, hatred, nationalism, and war? Yes, and always war and more war. You know, when we were kids it was "My daddy is bigger than your daddy" and now it's "My country is more powerful than your country." And of course there is always the ever present, "My God is better than your God and you don't believe in my God, therefore you are evil. Now, damn it, I have to kill you and don't you see, it's all your fault."

While Captain Marks and a new lieutenant were flying with the colonel, Jack was on a mission with two other new lieutenants. Colonel Simmons was going through his usual precarious routine and as usual was coming up empty handed. Stan was starting to feel sorry for the poor guy. It seemed as though he was out on a fishing expedition and could not catch a fish to save his life. But the guy just refused to quit.

The colonel told him that he was going to make a low pass just ahead and to his right and, once again, Stan remained airborne while watching the guy maneuver his aircraft. He did admire the colonel's flying ability; the old man could sure fly that thing. He watched as the plane descended and banked to its right while the colonel made observations of the area below. The first pass was completed; the colonel gained altitude and circled back for another pass. As he began to descend again, Stan observed what he thought may be movement on the ground and he followed the colonel. As he got closer, he did see something and transmitted, "Colonel, there is something down there."

As soon as he completed the transmission, he observed a flash from the ground and saw a projectile of some sort head directly toward the colonel's aircraft. It was a direct hit. The plane just disappeared before his eyes and a wide debris field descended to the ground.

Stan contacted TACP immediately and reported a downed aircraft at his location with enemy contact on the ground. He told the lieutenant in his flight to remain above and then descended toward the target. As he got closer, he saw another flash and veered sharply left. The projectile flew past the right side of his aircraft, and he then veered back toward the target. Another flash and he veered further right while this projectile went past his left side. This time, he was close to the target and as he banked to his left, fired 'Willie Petes,' and climbed away from the target area taking additional ground fire.

Fighter pilots checked in, reporting as a flight of two F-4s with napalm on board and target in sight. Stan did not believe there was any possibility that the colonel survived the incident but passed on the location of the downed aircraft in relation to the plumes of white smoke and told the pilots the direction from which they needed to approach the target area.

Captain Marks rejoined the other O-2 pilot in his former flight of three and watched the F-4 jockeys perform their fire dance. He was somewhat alarmed that he had become almost desensitized to the devastation he was about to witness. He was also upset about just having witnessed the death of his commanding officer. Another hero just joined the ranks of those to be memorialized by millions of Americans on Memorial Day and Veteran's Day.

During the flight back to Da Nang, Stan expressed a silent eulogy: *Thank you, Colonel Simmons. If it were not for people like you, we would not have all those wonderful holidays with parades and floats. We would not have all those backyard barbeques and pool parties. We would not have all those beach parties with hot dogs and beer. Thank you, Colonel Frank Simmons. You are indeed an American hero. You will be idolized and memorialized for the ages. Who knows, you may even get a footnote in a history book somewhere. Your name may be inscribed on a monument and, with any luck, we may even find enough of you down there to plant at the Arlington National Cemetery. Flags will be flown in your honor and one may even be placed on your grave annually. Thank you again for your service to your country, sir. I just wish I were certain that your ultimate sacrifice was for a very worthy cause.*

5

Stan was approaching his all-important DEROS and was starting to once again get that ole feeling of 'ants in his pants.' He was spending more time with Rich and his roommate, Don, since Jack was usually otherwise engaged. He had not heard much from Rich lately regarding his correspondence with the Aussie girlfriend and he did not intend to bring it up. That was none of his business and felt that it was probably best left alone. Rich had become more introspective of late and it made Stan wonder. He had heard some details about the stresses and strains endured by air traffic controllers at the RAPCON and he knew just how much he and his fellow pilots relied upon their expertise. He also wondered about how Rich viewed the conflict they had prepared for and were now engaged in for quite some time, but believed that was also best left alone. He could sense that they had both become more reflective and probably wanted to discuss the matter, but neither wished to stir up a hornets nest when the result would probably not be anything constructive.

Rich and Don often joined him at the gym and during his jogs around the main compound. He found them to be more thoughtful than most of the pilots he knew and he yearned for a more peaceful existence. *Funny,* he thought, he always wanted excitement in his life. He did not want what he thought of as a dreary existence, working a nine to five job day after day, week after week. But now, the life he discussed with Melanie on their R&R honeymoon/holiday sounded like heaven. He had never even considered teaching until she mentioned it to him and it now became an important goal. The only excitement he wanted now was to teach Adam how to ride a pony, go fishing with him and Melanie, and enjoy an occasional hunting trip with Mr. Blake. A nice occasional brandy, at night, on the front porch would be nice as well. Hell, when Adam got big enough, he would even take them to a nice summer rental at the Jersey shore and show them a good time at the boardwalk and the beach.

Letters from Abilene were starting to include more photographs of Adam and of progress on their new home. The frame was up and he was told that the goal was to have it complete for his homecoming. He was so fortunate, he thought. He never considered himself particularly bright or particularly good at anything; he was just an average guy who had to always work hard to accomplish anything at all. But he did always think of himself as lucky, and he'd take luck over good any day, he supposed.

Rich's DEROS was only a month or so after Stan's and they enjoyed discussing what life would be like when they returned home. Rich still had about a year left on his service commitment after he returned, was not sure if he would remain in the service, and was considering applying for a position with the FAA (Federal Aviation Administration). He was surprised to hear of Stan's decision, but said that he fully understood and thought teaching was a great idea.

Now that Jack. That Jack is a horse of an entirely different color. He showed up at the hooch one day raving about the

211

beautiful nurse he met from the German hospital ship just off the coast.

Her name was Helga and she was statuesque, according to Jack, with blonde hair and blue eyes. She even spoke a little English. The hospital ship was from the German Red Cross and provided medical services to Vietnamese civilians affected by the war.

"Jack, what happened to Mai Tai?" asked Stan.

"Oh, you mean Tai Wan. She's still around. Hell, Helga is a busy nurse and I can't see her that often. Now Tai, she says, 'Jack, you no butterfly me.' Hell, she's always there."

Stan smiled and replied, "Oh, gotcha."

No word on any replacement for Colonel Simmons yet and Captain Marks was not looking forward to working for another 'daredevil' commander. He flew his missions as he saw fit and advised the other guys to perform as he had been taught by Major Bannon. Major Bannon was still alive as far as he knew and Colonel Simmons was not. That was good enough reasoning for him, and it was a plan he fully intended to follow come hell or high water.

Rocket attacks during nighttime hours at the base were becoming ever more frequent. More and more, VNAF personnel were taking over functions formerly performed by American personnel. Fewer and fewer American faces and uniforms were seen on base and the level of base alert status was higher than ever. It was becoming more and more evident that it was time to "get the hell out of Dodge."

Time was getting short for Stan now and he was officially called a "short timer" by his fellow airmen. But he would never consider shirking his responsibilities, his 'duty.'

"Duty is the sublimest word in the English language." Robert E. Lee's words would be forever a part of his life. There was simply no escaping that concept.

We were trained at The Citadel by World War II and Korean War veterans, he thought. *We respected them and the sacrifices they made for their country and our way of life. We did, more so for the WWII veterans, however, but why? We as a nation were attacked at that time and most Americans supported the cause. We thought of our soldiers as outstanding human beings fighting for the causes of 'truth, justice, and, the American way.' Oh God, where have I heard that before? How in God's name does what we are doing now comport with such high ideals and motives?*

He recalled a conversation he once had with a classmate at college just prior to their graduation. That classmate was an Army 'brat' meaning that he was the son of a career military person and knew little of life outside military reservations. His father was an Army colonel stationed in Germany and he remarked that "Vietnam was a lousy war, but it's the only one we have. If we expect to get promotions, we've got to get there and show what we can do." That was a remark that he could not forget and thought about it often. He had been inspired by honorable men sent by their country's leadership to fight for honorable causes. He wanted very much to follow in those footsteps and feared he may have been misguided.

Five
Disarm

1

In another month or so, I'll be on the 'Freedom Bird' heading back to 'the world,' Stan thought as he proceeded on a northwesterly heading from Da Nang, with Jack as his wingman. It was another beautiful day in sunny I Corps and the words "GOOD MORNING VIETNAM" rang in his ears and put a smile on his face. The refrain from a well-known military radio broadcaster provided a much-needed link for 'in-country' personnel to familiar personalities back home.

He was really a 'short timer' now. Looking toward Jack's aircraft, they made eye contact, smiled, and gave each other a thumbs up. This they hoped would just be another of those routine, uneventful days permitting them to enjoy the beauty of their surroundings and the performance of the machines they had grown to love.

They took turns making low passes along portions of what they considered the probable course of the Ho Chi Minh Trail as they attempted to observe unusual activity. There was little need for verbal communication during the run. One of them would descend upon a suspected area to conduct a search and the other would observe from above. After rejoining the formation, the other would then take his turn.

After completing a run oriented in a northwesterly direction, they reversed course and proceeded on a southeasterly heading toward their airbase. It was then that they received notification of troops in contact south of their position needing air support. Captain Marks replied and they proceeded toward the reported location.

Approaching the scene, Stan Marks contacted the ground commander and was notified that the situation was dire. There was an overwhelming force attacking from the west and his troops had already taken many casualties. Stan relayed that information to TACP and he was notified that fighter aircraft would respond.

He then quickly coordinated with the ground officer regarding placement of his white phosphorous 'Willie Petes.' That settled, he gave a thumbs up to Jack and began his run toward the target area indicated as Jack observed from above. As he descended, he observed more than the usual ground activity and it became obvious that it was indeed a fairly large force firing upon friendlies.

The captain's aircraft then started to become a recipient of the opposing force's attentions. Increasingly heavy firepower was focused in his direction as he descended upon the target area and he took a few minor hits prior to launching his rockets. Almost simultaneously, a rather loud bang occurred at the front of his plane as he was violently jostled around the interior of the cockpit, causing him to temporarily lose control. At low altitude, that was extremely horrific. He was then able to regain enough control to level off just above treetops, but his front engine sputtered, smoked, and died. The ground fire continued, his windshield had already been shattered, and he noticed blood splatters in his cockpit. He needed to gain altitude and since his rear engine was still operating, he was able to control the craft with difficulty and gain altitude slowly. Ground fire continued and he felt sudden sharp pain in his right forearm, right hand, and right calf areas. Blood was at the right side of his face blurring his right eye vision.

Jack observed that his partner was in trouble and requested information regarding his condition. Stan was in pain and barely able to control his plane. He flew at low altitude back toward home base and the quality of his response to Jack revealed the extreme nature of his buddy's condition.

It was then that Jack took total charge. He told Stan that fighters were on their way to the target and that as soon as he cleared the area for the ground commander he would rejoin him for an escort home. A-1s came in, strafed the target area, followed by an F-4 napalm run. With rescue helicopters on the way and a secure LZ (Landing Zone), Jack proceeded toward the disabled aircraft. With both of his engines running at increased power, he was able to reach his comrade's slow moving plane without much delay.

As he approached the left side of the damaged aircraft, he became concerned about the low altitude of their flight and his observations of the plane caused him even greater concern. The nose of the plane was severely damaged and so was its nose gear. There was some smoke in the cockpit, holes in its fuselage, undercarriage, and some wing damage. He saw that Stan was not looking his way, appeared to be slouched over and staring straight ahead.

Jack transmitted to his pal and told him there was no need to respond if unable. He instructed him to key his mike twice if he was able to hear him. There was no immediate response, but the injured pilot did finally manage to key the mike twice. Jack realized that his friend was in trouble and that it was up to him to get him out of it somehow.

He transmitted to Stan, "Now listen, do not reply; just listen. You're a little too low. Pull up slightly."

The aircraft slowly ascended and he said, "Okay, good, now level off; your heading is good. I'm going to take the lead and you follow. We're going home. Key your mike twice if you can see ahead of your plane."

With much difficulty, he did key twice; however, there was a noticeable pause between each keystroke.

Jack contacted the control tower and notified them that a flight of two O-2s were inbound with an emergency condition. The first aircraft to land would be disabled with an engine out, damaged nose gear, broken windshield, and injured pilot. The second aircraft would execute a low approach and return for landing.

Stan was able to hear Jack's communication with the tower and was now fully aware of his situation. Thanks to Jack's observations, he knew what he had to do. But was he able? He was in pain and his vision was obscured. His right arm and hand were disabled and practically useless. *I've got to pull through somehow,* thought Stan. *I've come this far. Melanie and Adam are at home waiting for me and God damn it, I am not going to let them down. No, I won't. God, please help me. I have just got to do this somehow.*

They were on a VFR downwind leg to final approach. The flight was in view from the control tower and the air traffic controller relayed information regarding the aircraft's position to emergency personnel standing by.

Jack then transmitted, "Okay Stan, I know you heard all that. Now listen up, when we turn final, I'm going to drop back. You know about your nose gear situation and how to handle that. Everything is under control now. Just bring it home buddy, just bring it home."

Stan felt that he was about to pass out. He lost a lot of blood, and was barely able to see. He was feeling weak but knew he had to pull this off. This was it. This was his final exam. He had to pass.

It took more than everything he had to put those two main gear down on the pavement, but almost as soon as he did, he passed out. The aircraft's nose slammed down hard, sparks flew, and smoke appeared. The plane then veered to its left and exited the left side of the runway coming to final rest in a dirt and grass area.

Jack observed from above and was extremely anxious about what he had witnessed. He completed his pattern, landed his aircraft, taxied to the ramp, jumped in a jeep, and drove frantically toward his buddy's crippled machine. By the time he reached the plane, rescue personnel had already removed Stan from the aircraft and he appeared lifeless. They placed him in an ambulance and Jack hopped in with them. Medical personnel were working on him and Jack silently prayed. They took Stan's vital signs and a medic, noticing Jack's worried expression and tense demeanor, said, "Your friend is still alive. I think he'll make it."

2

Captain Marks remained unconscious, but his vital signs were good. He was a strong, young man and in excellent physical condition, however, the recovery period would extend to the end of this tour. His wounds were mostly confined to the right side of his body. Loss of blood was of initial concern, but that condition was now under control. The facial wounds were superficial, but did require stiches above his right eye. His eyesight would not be affected as a result of wounds sustained, but he would lose partial use of his right hand. That condition should improve somewhat with time and exercise, but he would no longer be able to fly as an Air Force pilot. The rest of his wounds were a result of shrapnel penetrations at his right hand, forearm, thigh, and calf. His flak jacket and helmet probably saved his life as evidenced by their condition after the fact.

Melanie was frantic when she was notified that her husband had been wounded; she felt desperate to see him. But, as soon as Stan was able, although still confined to bed rest, he wrote a letter to eliminate any doubt about his recovery. In that letter he explained that he would lose his flight status and would complete his commitment to the Air Force in a yet undetermined capacity; however, with his air traffic control and FAC training, he believed that he would be assigned air traffic control duties somewhere.

When Melanie received the letter, she was flooded with relief. Stan sounded like his old self; she decided to concentrate on the future and move forward. She was a bright young woman and was not about to let time spent as an Air Force personnel officer go to waste. Her contacts with personnel officers, still on active duty, may be beneficial and she was determined to use those contacts to advantage. Melanie explained Stan's position and the responses she received were very sympathetic. After all, he was a wounded pilot serving in a war zone; he had an infant child that he had not yet seen. He was a newlywed and he lost his flight status as a result of wounds suffered during combat. She asked that he be assigned to air traffic control duties as close as possible to their home in Texas.

The assistance was better than she anticipated. After a bit of research on the part of her associates, she was notified that he would be assigned to air traffic control officer duties at Dyess Air Force Base, Texas. Dyess is located approximately ten miles from their Abilene home and he would be able to commute to work. With receipt of that good news, she was thoroughly relieved and made plans for a joyous reunion.

3

Captain Marks did recover to a point where he could care for himself independently, although he did walk with a slight limp and was experiencing some difficulty using his right hand. Jack, Rich, Don, and the rest of his mates visited with regularity during the recovery period at the base infirmary, and he really appreciated the time they spent with him during that otherwise lonesome spell.

His 'Freedom Bird' was about to take him back to the homeland that was finally permitting him to gain re-entry after serving his required tour of duty. However, one more in-country affront needed to be endured prior to his flight back home. Drugs were considered a big problem stateside among the young population and, of course, many of America's youth were serving in Vietnam. A program called 'Operation Golden Flow' had been instituted to ensure that young folks serving in Vietnam were drug free before being permitted to return home. The program applied only to enlisted personnel and junior officers. Junior officers included lieutenants and captains. Stan was a captain and it was rather easy for him to comply with this new program since it was a simple matter of supplying a urine sample for testing, and he was already in a medical facility. However, most personnel needed to stand on line for long periods to submit their samples. When they reached the front of the line, they had to urinate into small containers while medical personnel confirmed that it was their sample. Those testing positive were required to undergo a period of rehabilitation prior to gaining re-admission to their homeland.

Captain Marks received his orders and boarded his flight back home. Lifting off the runway at Da Nang for the last time was an exuberant, yet uncomfortable, experience. So many thoughts raced through his mind as he viewed the runways and airfield slowly disappear while the plane climbed like the proverbial 'homesick angel.' A kaleidoscope of missions flown, friends lost to injury or death, joyful celebrations, letters written, news received from home, and hundreds of faces and expressions flowed through his mind as his fellow passengers cheered at a realization of a freedom they did not know they would ever live to see.

Seemed to him that he had just left the scene of an enormous family quarrel and that, as a stranger, he made the fatal error of becoming involved. He exited a bit battered and the battle still raged on despite his many attempts to bring about a resolution. *In the end it's the stranger that usually winds up the loser,* he thought. *Guess I should have minded my own business...that will teach me...I hope.*

It did not take very long at all. Shortly after any view of Vietnam was well behind him, his thoughtful expression turned to one of elation at the realization his next view of land would be Hawaii while en route to the U.S. mainland. He did it; he made it; the young, inexperienced Air Force lieutenant that flew to Vietnam one year ago was now returning as a veteran and as an Air Force captain. The joyful feeling at that moment made him proud of the accomplishment and especially proud that he had performed his 'duty.'

The majority of the soldiers on this commercial passenger aircraft, contracted for use by the Department of Defense, slept for most of the flight to Hawaii and were awakened by the flight crew announcement to prepare for landing. The last time Stan landed in Hawaii was for a thrilling R&R with Melanie terminating in a sorrowful goodbye prior to departing for the completion of his combat tour. This time, he thought, he would depart Hawaii, go home to see his entire family, and do his best to delete memory of the last year as quickly as possible. This stop in Honolulu was to refuel the aircraft, enjoy a scotch and water while waiting, and re-board for departure to his destination – Los Angeles, California, U.S.A.

En route to California, soldiers aboard the flight once again did as expected. They fell asleep. Only this time it was possible to detect slight smiles on their sleeping faces in sharp contrast to the dour, tenseness observed on flights inbound to the meat grinder.

Back in the United States, the soldiers deplaned and their bags were searched for illegal contraband prior to being allowed entry into the terminal areas. The bags were searched for drugs, weapons, or any items considered embarrassing to the military or governmental authorities back home. Seems that many returning soldiers had been filmed by news media attending anti-war protests wearing military paraphernalia. This aroused consternation among conservative groups. Broadcasts of military veterans opposed to the conflict were certainly not conducive to garnering support for current policy.

The veterans entering the terminal area encountered and mingled with a civilian population they had not seen in a year. They were required to wear military uniforms and that, of course, made them stand out in the crowd. Most of the soldiers needed to proceed to various ticket counters to board additional flights to their hometowns and as a result were scattering about the entire terminal area. The returning warriors were afforded half price standby tickets as long as they were in uniform and empty seats were available on flights departing to their destinations. These soldiers were not cheered, they were not welcomed home, there were no parades given in their honor, and in most cases, there was no one waiting to welcome them home unless they happened to reside in the Los Angeles area. The best they could hope for was to be totally ignored, which was not always the case.

Stan proceeded toward his ticket counter to arrange transportation from Los Angeles to Abilene. He was walking with a slight limp due to injuries and carried his small, carry-on luggage bag in his left hand to avoid discomfort in his injured right hand. As he approached his counter, an attractive young woman walking toward him glared and in an angry, clear voice sneered, "You murdering pig, you disgust me...looks like they managed to hurt you...good for them...they should have killed you." And she spit as she walked past. He did not stop; he continued toward his counter and as he looked around, it appeared that no one paid any attention to him or what had just transpired. *Welcome home you disgusting, murdering, pig,* he thought. *I did what I did thinking it was for your benefit, lovely lady. So sorry it did not work out that way.*

He checked in at the ticket counter and then tried to disappear as he awaited a boarding call. *Thank goodness he was heading to Texas,* he thought. *Once I board this flight, it will probably be different. After all, Texas is a military bastion teeming with conservative thought.*

Most people smiled at him and treated him as a welcome passenger aboard the flight to Abilene and he began to relax.

However, he did overhear a conversation between two men of approximately his age dressed in business attire. They touched on the current ongoing military situation and how many of their old friends' lives were drastically changed as a result. The men spoke of how smart people were able to avoid military service and how smart people had been profiting financially while others were 'getting all screwed up.'

All screwed up, he thought. *Am I missing something or am I now listening to those who are indeed screwed up? Isn't America the land of the free and the home of the brave because of those willing to give of themselves for the benefit of others? Our nation's leaders may not always make the right decisions, but that does not detract from the sacrifices of people following their nation's leadership. They had the strength of character to perform their 'duty.' And to Stan, there was simply nothing more honorable than the performance of one's 'duty.' I hope that what I'm listening to here is not indicative of the majority of our population. I guess they fail to realize that if ever brought to trial these smart folks will be judged by peers not smart enough to get excused from jury duty. Boy, now would that ever be poetic justice.*

Dismissing those people as fools, he thought of no one else but Melanie and his son, Adam. The thought of holding that precious little boy nearly brought tears to his eyes as he looked at the view outside the aircraft from his window seat. He then caught a glimpse of his own reflection in that window and studied what he saw. That reflection represents him now, he thought, but how does this guy compare to the Stan of last year? It was the Stan of last year that people had known and loved. How will they react to this year's Stan? Am I still the same person? Will anything change? Will I still know and love them? Will I be able to forget the horror of this war? And those who hate me for what I've done, will they ever forgive me for performing what I was told was my duty? Do I need forgiveness?

Mr. Blake met Stan at the airport. They gave each other big bear hugs, slapped each other's backs, and laughed with joy. *Boy, this sure beats Los Angeles,* he thought.

"Welcome home, son," said Mr. Blake. "The ladies are waiting at home for you. You know them – the preparations have been going on for days. Wait till you see that little boy of yours. He's a great little kid! Come on, let's go. My pickup truck is outside."

His father-in-law then took notice of Stan's limp and what appeared to be a slight deformity in his right hand, but didn't say a word about it.

They entered the truck, drove off, and stopped at the first available quiet intersection. The good ole retired history teacher reached over to his glove compartment and pulled out the same old flask. He handed it to Stan and said, "Have a swig, son."

Stan laughed and said, "With pleasure, sir. Thank you." He took a good long one and with a great big smile said, "You have no idea how much I appreciate that."

"I think I do, son. You have no idea how much I've been looking forward to giving it to you." And he took a great big swig himself.

It was apparent that Mr. Blake was overjoyed and that he was extremely proud of his son-in-law. The trip from the airport to the ranch was revitalizing. Stan felt as though he had been granted a new lease on life and as they drew nearer to the homestead, the long endured burden on his shoulders seemed to gradually diminish. They thoroughly enjoyed each other's company as the older gentleman filled him in on all the local happenings during his long absence.

As they drove along the winding, dirt road toward the Blake home, Stan observed a lone female figure on the front porch. He had imagined driving up to this house many times during the past year. In his visions, Melanie had always been running toward him with outstretched arms. But this was not her on that porch; it was her mother.

They walked toward the front porch and Mrs. Blake, noticing Stan's limp, ran toward him with open arms. They hugged each other, and she cried tears of joy saying, "Thank God you're home."

He looked back at the house and said, "Where's Melanie?"

Mr. Blake said, "Come with us, Stan. We want to show you something."

Mr. and Mrs. Blake led him along a pathway, around the left side of the house, and in the distance, he saw his new home.

"Oh, my God," he said. "It's just beautiful. Is this our home?"

"Yes, it is, son."

Then he saw his wife appear on the front porch of their new home holding baby Adam. He broke into a limping run toward Melanie and as he approached, he slowed down at the sight of something he did not expect to see. He continued his approach at a slower pace for a closer look and thought to himself. *Oh, my God, she's pregnant.*

He was within a few feet of her when he looked again with arms apart and wearing an enquiring expression.

Melanie said, "R&R? Hawaii? Remember? You big, beautiful, dummy."

Afterword

Their young grandson was excited as he looked up at the light aircraft flying at low altitude above them. "Grandpa, I'm going to ride a plane like that and do tricks like Daddy did. I'll do so many tricks!" Stan was amazed at the innocence and resiliency of the young boy. "Just be safe, son," he responded as he put his arm around his wife and tried to hide the emotions welling up inside him. There was a hole in their hearts that could never be filled.

Thoughts and visions of their son, Adam, invaded Stan's mind. That incredible little boy had grown into such a fine young man. Everything Adam did, from riding his first bike to flying his first plane, he did with extraordinary enthusiasm. He embodied a unique charisma, loved his fellow man, and wanted to change the world. Stan tried desperately to redirect his thoughts and stay focused on the present, but suddenly he could no longer hide the terrible feeling of sadness within him.

When will we ever learn? Will we ever learn? Will the madness ever end?

Another war, another 'duty,' another honorable life cut short. He looked up at the sky and with a heavy heart sighed, "We miss you, Adam."

***

Time is too slow for those who wait,
Too swift for those who fear,
Too long for those who grieve,
Too short for those who rejoice,
But for those who love, time is
Eternity.

— Henry Van Dyke

Although a work of historical fiction, the fact remains that the number of words in this entire volume falls somewhat short of the total number of American lives sacrificed during the Vietnam War.